# THE CRYPTIC CLUE

THE HEATHER REED MYSTERY SERIES 1

# THE CRYPTIC CLUE

## REBECCA PRICE JANNEY

WORD PUBLISHING
Dallas·London·Vancouver·Melbourne

Managing Editor : Laura Minchew
Project Editor: Beverly Phillips

**Library of Congress Cataloging–in–Publication Data**

Janney, Rebecca Price, 1957–
    The cryptic clue / Rebecca Price Janney.
        p.   cm.—(The Heather Reed mystery series ; #1) "Word kids!"
    Summary: When her neighbor Professor Samra mysteriously disappears, sixteen-year-old Heather Reed tries to find out what has happened to him and discovers a CIA agent involved with terrorists.
    ISBN 0–8499–3834–1
    [1. Mystery and detective stories.]  I. Title.  II. Series : Janney, Rebecca Price, 1957–  Heather Reed mystery series ; #1.
PZ7.J2433Cr   1993
[Fic]—dc20                            92–45185
                                        CIP
                                        AC

*Printed in the United States*

3 4 5 6 7 8 9 LBM 9 8 7 6 5 4 3 2 1

*This book is dedicated to Jeremy Clyde, who inspired it; my husband, Scott, who helped bring it to life; and Brian McElhinney, whom I remember with affection.*

# Contents

# 1

## A Rude Awakening

"I can't wait to see Dr. Samra!" sixteen-year-old Heather Reed exclaimed, walking across the Kirby College campus.

Her best friend Jenn McLaughlin agreed. "He's only been gone four months, but it seems so much longer."

Heather's parents had picked up the famous history professor at Philadelphia International Airport the night before. Dr. George Samra enjoyed popularity with students and fame for his books about the Middle East. He had spent the entire fall term in the Middle East writing a new book on terrorism.

The Samras were like family to Heather. She had lived next door to them since she was a baby.

Heather and Jenn walked in the cold from Brian Reed's dorm to the professor's office. Heather's brother was moving his things back to the campus following Christmas vacation. The girls had gone along to help unload the car and to visit Dr. Samra.

When they reached the arts and sciences building, Heather and Jenn climbed the old steps to the History Department. But as they neared Dr. Samra's office, they heard shouting.

"I said 'No!'" Dr. Samra yelled.

"That's just fine!" a younger professor roared.

Then both men stomped into their offices. The doors slammed, filling the hall with an angry echo. Heather and Jenn stood staring in disbelief.

"What was that all about?" Heather exclaimed.

"I don't know!" Jenn admitted, shocked by the outburst. "Who was the other guy?"

"Horrible Hal Morgan," Heather said, making a face. "No wonder Brian hated his class." She grew thoughtful. "I wonder what made them so furious with each other?"

"Maybe Dr. Samra found out how poorly Morgan did substituting for him," her friend suggested.

"Let's find out." Heather moved toward the door to Dr. Samra's office, but Jenn held back.

"I say we go back to Brian's dorm," she suggested. "Maybe we shouldn't bother Dr. Samra."

Heather's hazel eyes twinkled. "Can't wait, huh?"

Her red-headed friend blushed. Jenn had had a crush on Brian Reed since she was in second grade. That's when the McLaughlin's had moved into the house across the street from the Reeds and Samras.

"I'm going to see him," Heather decided stubbornly. "If you'd rather see Brian, I'll tell Dr. Samra hello for you."

Jenn squared her broad shoulders and lifted her chin. "I have my pride, you know. I will not throw myself at your brother."

"Good. Let's go." Heather gently shoved her toward the professor's door, then knocked loudly.

"Come in," he called out wearily.

They entered the room, but their friend was nowhere in sight.

"Dr. Samra, where are you?" Jenn called out.

His gray head peeked out from behind a mountain of mail on his desk.

"Buried alive, eh?" Heather joked.

"Ah, my dear little friends," he said, getting up to hug them. He still called them "little" no matter how grown-up they had become. "I told Mrs. Greenberg to sort my mail." He sighed. "No one listens to me anymore."

*I wonder what he means,* Heather thought. "We were helping Brian move back and thought we'd stop by. Want some help?" She moved toward the desk, but he put up a hand to stop her.

"Not today." The plump man looked down at the floor littered with stacks of papers. "Your offer tempts me, though. Just look at that mess! Those are term papers and exams from last spring." He sighed again.

"Please let us help," Heather begged.

"No," he said firmly. "I need to be alone." He forced a smile. "Thank you just the same."

"Maybe you should go home and rest," she suggested. "You seem really bummed out."

"I do?" A strange look came into his dark brown eyes then quickly disappeared. "It's only jet lag."

Heather wasn't convinced but didn't push him. "Okay, but when you've rested up, I want to hear all about your trip. Your letters didn't say much," she teased.

"I need to get back to work," Dr. Samra said abruptly. "Tomorrow is Wednesday already, the beginning of the spring semester, and I'm way behind."

"Don't push yourself too hard," Jenn cautioned him.

"Let me know if I can help," Heather offered. She was still a bit puzzled by his reluctance to accept her help. During summer vacations, she often did secretarial work for the professor. But she had never seen him so tense. She tried to catch his eye, but the professor quickly looked away.

Heather knew something wasn't right and didn't want to leave. But Jenn poked her. "Let's go," she said firmly. This time her adventurous friend listened.

As they walked slowly back to Brian's dorm, Heather said, "Something smells rotten in Kirby."

Jenn nodded. "I never heard him yell before."

"I haven't either. Though I've given him plenty of reasons!" Heather laughed.

"Remember when we stayed overnight at the Samras when we were twelve?" Jenn asked. "You saw something that looked like a soda bottle in the bathroom."

"And I drank it before realizing it was cola bubble bath!" Heather laughed out loud. But she quickly became serious again. "Dr. Samra wouldn't get angry over a little thing. Whatever is bothering him must be important."

After getting Brian settled, the girls left. At Heather's house she found her parents in the kitchen fixing dinner. Because of their busy schedules, they often worked together on meals. Mr. Reed was the managing editor of *The Philadelphia Journal,* and Mrs. Reed, a popular pediatrician, kept a home office.

"Did you get Brian situated?" Heather's mother asked in her native South Carolina accent.

"Yes. But not Dr. Samra. He was pretty unsettled," the teenager said. She explained what had happened.

"He was exhausted last night," her father explained simply as he stirred a pot of vegetable soup.

Heather wasn't so sure. Her concern intensified when Mrs. Samra called at seven-thirty that evening saying her husband hadn't come home yet. After calling Jenn on the phone and doing her homework, Heather went to bed at ten. Her mother awakened her an hour later.

"The police chief is here with the head of security from Kirby College," she said tensely. "They want to talk to you."

"Mom, I didn't do anything. Honest!" Heather defended.

"It's about Dr. Samra," her mother said. "Get dressed and come downstairs."

She quickly got out of her pink nightshirt and into the black stirrup pants and over-sized sweater she had laid out for school the next day.

"Hello, Heather," Chief Andrew Cullen said. He stood when she entered the living room. "Sorry to wake you up." Then he introduced her to Bob Rizzo from the college security department, and they all sat down.

"What's going on?" Heather asked.

Chief Cullen took a deep breath. "Dr. Samra has disappeared."

# 2

# The Missing Professor

Heather listened in stunned silence as Mr. Rizzo told the Reeds what happened.

"When Mrs. Samra called us about 7:45 P.M., we searched the campus and found Professor Samra's car—but not him."

The police chief picked up the story. "Mrs. Samra said she last spoke with her husband just after noon today. He mentioned you and your friend Jenn McLaughlin had just left his office."

"That's right," Heather nodded. She had known something was wrong when she'd seen the professor earlier.

"How long did you talk to him?" he asked.

"Maybe five minutes."

"Did you see him at all after that?" he pursued.

"No. We went back to Brian's dorm."

Chief Cullen looked very concerned. "Since Dr. Samra just got back from the Middle East, we figured we'd better look into this right away. With the work he does on terrorism, well . . ." He paused, a look of concern on his face. "We're going to list him as missing." He sipped coffee Mrs. Reed had served before Heather came downstairs. "When you saw him, Heather, who else was around?"

"I only saw one other professor," she said.

"Who?"

"Dr. Morgan."

"He's the man who taught Dr. Samra's courses while he was away in the fall," Mr. Reed explained.

"Did you talk to this man?" Cullen questioned Heather.

"No," she said, "but Dr. Samra was speaking to him right before Jenn and I arrived."

"I see," the police chief said. "Was there anything unusual about the way Dr. Samra acted?" The heavy-set man leaned back in the dainty chair. It creaked under his weight. Out of politeness the Reeds pretended not to notice.

Heather proceeded. "Yes, there was. He argued with Dr. Morgan in the hallway. And when I talked to him later, Dr. Samra was cranky. I knew the trip had wiped him out, but there seemed more to it than that. I think Dr. Morgan upset him."

"That is strange," Chief Cullen said. "I know the doc pretty well. He seems to get along with everyone. Still, when your business is the Middle East . . ." He gave a low whistle.

"Can we do anything?" Mrs. Reed asked.

Chief Cullen frowned. "Heather was probably one of the last people to see the professor before his disappearance. We may need to talk to her again."

"That would be fine," her mother consented.

"For sure," Heather agreed eagerly. "You let me know if I can help in any way. Of course, Jenn saw him too."

"We're going over there now," Chief Cullen said.

After the officers left, the Reeds said a prayer together for Dr. Samra's safety. They talked awhile longer about the day's events, then Heather went back to bed. But she lay wide awake with her excited thoughts. On the one hand, the news of Dr. Samra's disappearance stung. *He might be in danger this very minute,* she considered. *Or worse.* On the other hand, she enjoyed being in the thick of the situation. She wanted to help find her missing friend.

*But why,* she kept wondering, *would he just disappear? Did someone kidnap him, or did he simply vanish?* For the time being, Heather refused to think of other, even more unpleasant, possibilities.

By Wednesday morning the professor still hadn't come home. Heather and Jenn discussed the mystery on the way to school.

"Can you believe it?" Jenn asked.

"Yes and no," Heather replied. "Yes, because I knew something wasn't quite right when we saw him. No, because I honestly am shocked."

The two sixteen-year-olds found it difficult to think about anything else the whole day. They each hoped their teachers had read the morning papers or heard the news on the radio. Maybe then they wouldn't require too much of them.

During a study period, Heather called her mother's office to see if she knew anything further. She did.

"Someone ransacked Dr. Samra's campus office late last night," she reported.

"Was the person caught?" Heather's heart raced.

"No. And nothing seemed to be stolen."

Heather spent the rest of the school day trying to decide what kind of link there could be between the professor's disappearance and the office break-in. Somehow the events didn't seem to fit. *If someone kidnapped him, why would they break into his office now?* she pondered. *Wouldn't they have done that first, especially if that's where he was captured? It would be terribly risky to go back.*

On the way home after school, Jenn said she thought Dr. Samra had been kidnapped. "He wouldn't just run away," she stated firmly. But she, too, had trouble making sense out of the break-in.

When she got home, Heather found a note saying her mother was making a hospital call. So she went to the family room to sit quietly and think. Lying on the large coffee table was a copy of *The Philadelphia Journal.* That meant her father had come home because he always brought a paper with him. She saw the headline, "Kirby Professor Disappears," and plopped down on the couch to read the article.

Just as she finished reading it, Heather's dad entered the room. He was wearing his usual conservative suit and loud-colored socks. "Do you know anything more?" she asked hopefully.

"I'm afraid not," he said, looking upset.

"Dad, if someone kidnapped Dr. Samra, wouldn't there have been signs of a struggle?" she asked.

He scratched his head thoughtfully and sat on the couch. "Probably. But when I spoke with Chief Cullen this morning, he said there hadn't been a fight in the office. And whoever broke in later just scattered things as though they were searching for something. They didn't even mess up the lock."

"You mean they had a key?" Heather asked, wide-eyed. "That could mean someone who works with Dr. Samra did the job?"

"Hmm. That doesn't seem likely," Mr. Reed commented. "Maybe the person is simply an expert lock-picker."

"I'm more confused than ever," she sighed.

Her father got up and gave her a little hug. "I'm going next door to check on Miriam. I'm sure she must be quite troubled. You look tired from staying up so late last night. How about a nap?"

Suddenly she felt drained. "That sounds good," Heather agreed. She stretched out on the couch, pulling a light-weight afghan over her. In minutes she was sound asleep.

A half hour later the front doorbell rang, but no one answered it. Still groggy, Heather got up and made her way to the living room. *Hardly anyone uses this door,* she thought, giving it an extra tug. When she opened it, there stood a well-dressed man in his thirties.

"Hello. Are you Heather Reed?" he asked politely.

"Yes," she answered.

"I came to speak with you." He opened a wallet and presented a badge. "I'm Special Agent Peter Roselmann of the FBI," he announced.

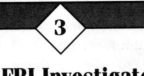

# 3

# The FBI Investigates

Heather's jaw dropped. "Come in," she said, holding the door open for him. "Please sit down."

The serious-looking agent sat opposite the teenager. Heather was feeling uneasy. She wished her father had not gone next door.

"I'm investigating George Samra's disappearance," he explained. "The police told me you were one of the last people to see him."

"That's right, but why is the FBI investigating?" she questioned.

Roselmann inhaled deeply. "The Kirby Police Department contacted us because of the professor's trip to the Middle East. There may be a connection."

"I'd like to get my father and my best friend, if you don't mind," Heather requested.

"Please do," Roselmann consented.

Heather quickly tracked them down on the phone. Mr. Reed returned from the Samras', and Jenn hurried across the street from her home. Then Roselmann began.

"We believe someone may have kidnapped Dr. Samra and is holding him hostage."

*How can he act so calm?* Heather marveled. Jenn started crying, and Mr. Reed put an arm around her shoulder.

"We're very close to him," Heather explained.

"I see," Roselmann commented unemotionally. "Miss Reed, please describe your relationship with Dr. Samra."

"I've known him all my life," she said. "My parents are from South Carolina. All our relatives live there, so the Samras are a second family to us. My brother even goes to Kirby College because of Dr. Samra."

Roselmann raised an eyebrow. "You have a brother at Kirby?"

"Yes," Mr. Reed cut in. "Brian's a freshman."

The agent nodded. "Suppose you tell me everything you can remember about your visit yesterday."

Heather glanced in Jenn's direction. Her friend blew her nose, trying to get her tears under control.

"We went to the college to help Brian move back to the dorm and to visit Dr. Samra," Heather began. "When we got to the history department, he was arguing with another professor."

"Could you hear what they were saying?" he asked.

"Uh huh. Dr. Samra shouted, 'I said no.' Then Dr. Morgan—the other professor—yelled, 'Well, that's just fine!'"

"Then what happened?"

"They stormed into their offices," Heather concluded.

Jenn found her voice. "Yeah, they slammed the doors so hard, I thought the windows would break."

"What do you know about Dr. Morgan?" he asked.

Mr. Reed explained, "He taught Dr. Samra's classes in the fall. My son had him, and to be honest, he didn't like the guy. Neither did the others."

"Is he a faculty member?" asked the agent.

"His contract is just for this year," Mr. Reed said.

"What makes him so unpopular?" Roselmann asked, making notes in a small book.

"Brian says he's a real tyrant," Heather cut in. "He gives them more homework than any of the other professors. Plus he acts like A's come out of his paycheck. Brian only got a B from him—he got A's in all his other classes."

"Did anything else seem odd to you yesterday?" Roselmann questioned.

"Yes, as a matter of fact, Dr. Samra was real grumpy. At the time, Jenn and I figured he was just tired."

Roselmann's eyes rested on Heather momentarily as if trying to read some clue in her face.

"Could Dr. Morgan have something to do with the professor's disappearance?" she asked.

"It's too soon to tell," he said. He got up to go. "Thank you for your time and help," he told the trio.

"Isn't there anything else we can do?" Heather asked. "I'd love to help find Dr. Samra."

Jenn didn't say anything. She didn't want to get involved with the FBI.

"Uh, no thanks," he struggled not to laugh. "Mr. Reed, I understand you were just visiting Mrs. Samra?"

"That's right," he agreed.

"Good. That's my next stop."

"I'll take you there," Heather exclaimed, jumping up.

"I can find it myself," Roselmann chuckled.

"No problem," she insisted, snatching her jacket from the hall closet. Heather looked eagerly at Jenn.

"I'd better go home," she said. "We should be eating soon."

"That's fine," Roselmann said. After all he didn't need three people to show him the house next door.

"I'll talk to you later," Heather called after her friend, who left quickly.

The Reeds and Samras lived in a quiet neighborhood. But now reporters filled the Samras' front lawn. Mr. Reed hurried next door to restore order, amazed at how quickly they had gathered. Some curious neighbors stared from their yards and porches.

"Please listen," Patrick Reed pleaded. "Mrs. Samra is in no condition to give interviews."

Roselmann shoved through the throng and went up to Heather's father. "Where did your daughter go?"

They strained to find her in the crowd but couldn't. At five-feet-two inches, Heather wouldn't be easy to spot in this mob.

"Hey, who are you?" a newswoman demanded, pushing a microphone toward Roselmann's face.

He ignored it and lifted his voice above the murmur of journalists. "Look, people, if you don't leave, I'll arrest every one of you for trespassing."

He handled himself with such authority that no one challenged him. Within minutes, the crowd scattered.

"I'm a newspaperman, so I figured they'd listen to me," Mr. Reed explained as they headed toward the Samras' door. "I was wrong," he smiled sheepishly.

They entered the house through a pleasant hallway lined with family portraits. Patrick Reed led the agent to the family room where Mrs. Samra sat on a couch flanked by her daughter, Karen, and Heather.

"There you are!" Mr. Reed exclaimed.

"I snuck in through the back door," Heather said.

The professor's wife, normally a strong and dignified woman, appeared tense and fearful. "Pat, did you get rid of those dreadful people? They arrived just after you left."

"Actually, *he* did," Heather's dad admitted, pointing to Roselmann. "Miriam Samra, this is, um—I'm terribly sorry, but I've forgotten your name."

"Peter Roselmann," the agent said, walking across the room to shake the woman's trembling hand. "I'm with the FBI."

She looked surprised. "It's, uh, nice to meet you. This is our youngest daughter, Karen. And this is our special friend, Heather Reed, Pat's girl."

"We've met. May I sit down?"

"Yes, of course, Mr., uh . . . what did you say your last name was again?"

"Roselmann," he repeated patiently.

"You must disregard my manners, Mr. Roselmann. I'm under a terrible strain."

"I understand. Do you feel up to answering some questions?" he inquired.

"I suppose," she answered uncertainly.

"Mrs. Samra, did you visit your husband in the Middle East?"

"No. That would be dangerous. You see, George is from Lebanon, so he blends in. I would just confuse the matter. What's more, our oldest daughter just had a baby, so I spent a few months with her."

"What type of research was your husband doing?"

"He's working on a book about terrorism," she said. *That sounds really bad!* Heather thought.

Roselmann frowned. "That's a grave matter, Mrs. Samra. He may be involved on the wrong side."

"I beg your pardon! My husband is an upstanding Christian," she objected angrily.

# 4

## A Possible Lead

Tension filled the room, but Special Agent Roselmann continued. "Did Dr. Samra do anything unusual when he returned from his trip?"

It was becoming more difficult for Mrs. Samra to talk to this man. She looked in Mr. Reed's direction for guidance. He encouraged her to share what she knew. "He was rather quiet," she said. "And he stayed in his study for quite a while."

Roselmann jotted down the information, then tapped his pen against his teeth. "Do you know why?"

She did know but again she realized it sounded bad. "He was working on his laptop computer."

The FBI agent jumped on this. "That doesn't sound like an exhausted man to me," he remarked.

"Well, he was," Mrs. Samra defended.

"Very well," Roselmann said. "What was he doing?"

The professor's wife nervously fingered her pearl necklace. George Samra's actions had seemed so innocent at the time. "He didn't tell me, but I assumed it had something to do with his book or his spring classes. I'm sure there was nothing else to it."

"You said he has a study?" the tall agent asked.

"Yes," she answered.

"I'd like to look around if you don't mind."

"All right," Mrs. Samra said stiffly. She and Mr. Reed led Roselmann down the hall to an oak-paneled room. Wooden shelves bulged with hundreds of books.

"Is that computer here?" he asked.

She shook her head. "He must have taken it to school with him. Normally he keeps it at home."

The agent started picking up items on the desk. He ignored Mrs. Samra. Mr. Reed took her lightly by the elbow. "Let's go back to the family room."

"But . . ." she protested.

"I'm sure it's all right," he told her.

The small group waited anxiously for Roselmann to return. When Mrs. Samra could take it no longer, she announced, "I'm going to make a pot of tea."

"I'll help," her daughter volunteered.

"That makes another Samra I've never seen so upset before," Heather whispered to her dad.

"What do you mean?"

"The way she yelled at Mr. Roselmann."

"I'm sure you can understand it, Heather," her father said. "This is serious."

"He could be nicer to her," Heather criticized.

"FBI agents aren't trained to be friendly," Mr. Reed commented.

Twenty minutes later, Heather knocked lightly on the open door of the study to get Roselmann's attention. "Are you almost finished?"

The agent put down a book he'd been studying closely and asked, "Does Dr. Samra know Greek?"

Heather looked at the volume. "Yes. That's his New Testament. He uses it for devotions."

"Excuse me?" Roselmann looked puzzled.

"Devotions," she repeated. "He reads the Bible every day in Greek."

"What for?" he asked.

It was Heather's turn to look puzzled. "Because he's a Christian, and Christians read the Bible. He likes reading it in Greek because the New Testament was written in that language."

"Oh." He made a face and laid the Bible on the desk. "Sounds pretty strange to me."

Over cups of tea and a tray of cookies, Peter Roselmann shared his thoughts about the professor's disappearance. "I'm just guessing now, testing every possible angle. On the one hand, Dr. Samra may be a hostage. However, there's been no call or note demanding a ransom. On the other hand, he may be part of a terrorist group himself. Then of course, he may simply have just skipped town."

"George is a good man," Mrs. Samra insisted as tears filled her eyes. "He wouldn't do anything wrong. And why would someone kidnap him?"

"I don't think he'd simply disappear," Mr. Reed added.

"That's not like him. He is one of the most honest and decent men I have ever known."

Roselmann tried not to argue. "I hear you. But just in case he did leave of his own free will, where might he go?"

Mrs. Samra glared at him. "He wouldn't do that."

"Look at it this way," the agent said, "he may be trying to avoid someone."

Then Heather had an inspiration. "Maybe he went to Cape May! Our families have summer homes there."

He looked interested. "That would make sense."

"Mr. Roselmann, I don't have school tomorrow because of a teacher's in-service day, and my brother doesn't have Thursday classes. We could take you there. We'd know exactly where to look for him." Her face lit up with excitement, but not for long. . . . Roselmann was not interested in her help. He said he would have the Cape May police investigate. The teenager's hopes were dashed.

"If you need to get in touch with me, Mrs. Samra, here is my beeper number," the agent said, handing her his card. "I have upset you, and I apologize for that. I know you believe in your husband. But consider what I've been told: an expert on terrorism disappears the day after returning from the Middle East."

She appreciated the gesture. "Thank you, Mr. Roselmann." Trusting him a bit more now, she dared to ask, "Do you think my husband is still alive?" Her lips trembled.

"I hope so, Mrs. Samra. But he may have enemies who don't want to keep it that way," he said.

"But everyone likes George," she protested.

"Not everyone," Roselmann corrected. "On the day he disappeared, your husband had a heated argument with another professor."

"With whom?" she demanded.

"Dr. Hal Morgan."

Her gray-blue eyes flashed. "That doesn't surprise me in the least," she said bitterly. "He pestered my husband the whole time George was abroad, calling him and writing letters."

"About what?" Roselmann looked very interested.

"George's new book. Hal Morgan knows that the publishing house expects it to be an important bestseller. Do you want to know what I think?" She didn't wait to find out. "Dr. Morgan wanted to get rid of George in order to steal the manuscript!"

# 5

## What Next?

Heather went home and moped. "I want to go to Cape May," she complained to her pet rabbit Murgatroid. "If Dr. Samra is there, I could find him." The black and white Dutch bunny regarded her sympathetically.

After dinner that evening, Heather cleared the table and loaded the dishwasher. Then she worked half-heartedly on an English assignment. First she doodled in the margins. Then she twirled a piece of hair around her finger. Suddenly Heather clamped her notebook shut and ran downstairs. Grabbing her leather bomber jacket, she headed for the door. "Mom! Dad!" She called over her shoulder to her parents, "I'm going over to Brian's."

"What for?" her mother asked, looking up from a puzzle on the coffee table.

"He'll be dying to know what happened," she explained.

"You mean you're dying to tell him," her dad teased. "Don't be late."

Heather didn't tell them she'd had one of her brainstorms. She stopped at Jenn's house and asked her to come along.

It took them fifteen minutes to drive across town to Kirby College. When they entered Brian's colonial-style dorm, Heather and Jenn saw his roommate, Joe Rutli, watching TV in the lounge.

"Hi, Heather! Jenn! Looking for Brian?" the friendly young man said with a wave.

"Yes, we are," Heather replied. "Is he around?"

"Nope. He went to the library. Buried in the books as usual," Joe answered.

Brian Reed, a dean's list student, took his studies very seriously. He wanted to follow in his mother's footsteps. In spite of being a bookworm, however, Brian had many friends.

"Thanks." Heather and Jenn turned to leave.

"Hey," Joe called out, "that's too bad about Dr. Samra. Have you heard any more news about him?"

"Nothing yet," the petite teen responded.

The girls headed for the library on the other side of the well-lighted campus. Frosty air nipped at their gloved hands and bare faces. At the four-story library, Heather suggested starting on the bottom floor and working their way up. They finally found him on the second floor working on a biology lesson.

Brian's brown eyes sparkled. He laid the book down, marking his place with a finger. "I heard you were at the Samras' with the FBI. What gives, Heather?"

"How did you know?" she asked.

"News travels, little sister." Brian smiled impishly. "Actually I bumped into Marybeth Davis in the cafeteria, and she started flapping her gums about some drop-dead, good-looking government agent who was at the house."

"Come to think of it, I saw her mother gaping from across the street," Jenn said in disgust.

"A bunch of reporters gathered on the lawn trying to get an interview, and Mr. Roselmann, the FBI agent, cleared them out," Heather explained.

Then she told Brian about their meeting with Roselmann. "And now I really need to talk to you both about something," she said excitedly. "You see . . . "

Brian cut her off. "Whoa! I'll listen, but you caught me at a critical part of this assignment. Give me fifteen minutes, then meet me at the main entrance. We can go to the campus center and talk."

Although Heather wanted to tell him right away, she understood. "No problem. We'll see you in a bit."

"What's the big secret?" Jenn asked when they walked away.

"You'll see," she smiled.

"I thought I was your best friend," Jenn whined.

To pass the time they browsed through the magazine area. When Heather got to the "M's," a certain publication caught her eye—*Middle East Today*. She sat on a nearby chair and started to read while Jenn curled up next to her with a fashion magazine.

In the table of contents Heather was amazed to read, "NEW DISCOVERIES ON TERRORISM by Dr. Harold B. Morgan!" She quickly turned to the article and began reading, surprised by the similarity to Dr. Samra's recent studies.

*Maybe Mrs. Samra is right!* she thought.

After the article it said, "Harold B. Morgan, an expert on terrorism, is an adjunct history professor at Kirby College, Kirby, PA. He is currently writing a book about terrorism."

*She is right!* Heather concluded silently. *I'll bet he is trying to steal Dr. Samra's research. But is Horrible Hal also responsible for his disappearance? What if he kills Dr. Samra?* she worried. The terrible thought sent shivers down her spine. She quickly made a copy of Morgan's story. Then she showed Jenn.

"What a rotten trick!" she exclaimed.

Heather couldn't wait to tell Brian about the article. The girls met him a few minutes later and, over sodas and French fries, told him first about their meeting with the FBI agent. Then Heather showed Brian the copy of Hal Morgan's magazine article. As her brother read it, she watched his eyes fill with anger.

"I don't know what other evidence you need," he said.

Then Heather shared her plan with him and Jenn. "Let's go to Cape May tomorrow," she began. "If Dr. Samra is hiding, maybe he went there, but not to his house. Then how would the police know where to look? We could check not only the cottage, but also his hangouts. Plus we could question his friends. Jenn and

I don't have any classes tomorrow because of the teachers' in-service day."

Brian knew this was another of his sister's hairbrained schemes. "Both the FBI agent and Dad told you not to go there," he said with irritation. "You're always getting into trouble because you don't listen."

"You're telling me!" Jenn rolled her eyes.

"Like when?" Heather challenged.

"Like the time Mom sent us to the store and warned us not to go across Mr. Vitelli's field. But you insisted it was the best way, and we fell in a cesspool."

"I was eight years old, Brian!" she protested.

"Okay, what about last year, right before you got your driver's license?" he pursued. "You got impatient waiting for me and the folks to teach you how to drive. So you took the car by yourself and wiped out Dr. Samra's flower garden."

"We're not talking about cesspools or flower gardens," she argued. "Something terrible may have happened to Dr. Samra, and we can help."

He tried another method. "The campus police found Dr. Samra's car in the faculty lot."

"I know that," Heather shot back.

"So how did he get to Cape May?" her brother challenged.

"There are other ways," she claimed. Heather picked up a French fry, then tossed it back.

Jenn didn't say anything. She knew better than to get involved in a brother-sister fight—especially when the brother was Brian Reed.

The Kirby freshman asked, "You think we could do a better job of finding Dr. Samra than the police and the FBI?" His voice was full of doubt.

"Yes, and I told you why." Heather refused to back down. "The police don't know where he might be."

"They have ways of finding out, though," he added. But when Brian saw Heather's disappointed look, he caved in. "Okay, okay. I'll go, even though it's a waste of time. And if I don't, you'll talk Jenn into it, and the two of you will get into all kinds of trouble." When Heather began to thank him, he held up a hand to stop her. "I want to check something first." He reached into his pocket and took out his key chain. "What do you know? I still have a key to the Samras' cottage. They gave it to me last summer so I could check on the place while they went away for a few weeks."

"Terrific!" Heather exclaimed. "Oh, Brian, can't you see—this means we're supposed to go!"

He and Jenn burst out laughing.

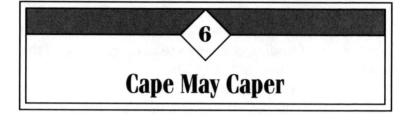

# 6

## Cape May Caper

Heather immediately started planning for Thursday's trip. "Let's take a recent picture of Dr. Samra to show people," she encouraged. "I'll bet Joe has one."

Brian's roommate served as a school photographer and had access to faculty pictures.

"I'll ask," her brother promised.

"Great! We'll pick you up at nine-thirty tomorrow morning in the dorm parking lot."

Brian and Heather shared a small red sedan. And since the college didn't allow freshman to have cars on campus, Heather kept the vehicle at home.

"That sounds good," her handsome brother agreed.

"I'm so glad you're going to help!" exclaimed Heather. "Just think—we might find Dr. Samra!"

When she got home later, Heather found her dad in the family room.

"Where's Mom?" she asked.

"Seeing a child with an ear infection." He closed the book he had been reading and set it aside.

"Wait 'til you see this!" Heather shouted. She showed her dad Hal Morgan's article then got comfortable on the couch as he scanned it.

"I'm going right over to tell Miriam about this," he said getting up from his recliner. "This agrees with what she told that Roselmann fellow."

"Will you tell him, too?" Heather asked.

"Yes, I believe I will," Mr. Reed said. I'm convinced Dr. Samra is innocent."

At breakfast Thursday morning Heather felt so excited she could hardly eat. Fortunately her parents seemed too distracted to notice. When they left for their offices, Heather quickly collected a flashlight, pocketknife, matches, and some food. Then the sixteen-year-old met Jenn outside.

"Boy, it's cold!" Jenn said, clapping her hands together.

As they climbed into the red car, Heather asked, "Why don't you wear warmer clothes?"

"Maybe for the same reason you can't stay out of trouble," her friend teased.

"You win!" Heather laughed, backing out of the driveway. She also turned on the radio. The teenagers learned that light snow had fallen at the New Jersey shore overnight.

"That shouldn't interfere with our trip," Heather said, relieved.

When they reached Brian minutes later, he looked doubtful. His sister was afraid he might change his mind. "I have a funny feeling about this," he complained.

"Everything will be all right," Heather said, trying not to get annoyed. "Trust me."

Although her brother and Jenn laughed at the remark, they didn't make further protests.

"Did you bring the picture?" Heather asked.

"Yeah. Joe got me a good head shot," Brian announced, showing them an excellent photograph.

The young people encountered only light traffic on their way to the shore. The morning rush hour had thinned out. As the scenes changed from suburbs and shopping malls to pine trees and sandy soil, Heather's excitement grew. The squawking sea gulls seemed to cheer them on. They reached the outskirts of the resort town at eleven-thirty.

"Let's go directly to the Samras'," Heather suggested. Although she felt hungry, the teenager couldn't imagine delaying their mission.

"You're the leader," Brian conceded. "By any chance, did you bring food?"

His sister pointed to her pack. "I put some bananas and peanut butter crackers in there."

"And I brought a container of hot chocolate," Jenn added.

They ate the snacks as Heather drove over the bridge to the Victorian town. Then she headed to Cape May Point where both the Reeds and Samras had summer homes.

When they neared the Samras' street, they noticed only a few cars. Just a few year-round residents lived there. Most of the sidewalks were lightly covered with snow.

"I'll park a block away to avoid detection," Heather announced.

Then the trio got out of the car and quietly approached the Samras' white house with green shutters.

Suddenly Brian whispered, "Look over there!" He pointed out two sets of footprints leading to the house. When they looked more closely, they noticed only one pair led back outside.

"What do we do now?" Jenn was both thrilled and scared all at once.

"I'll go in first," Brian said. "If anything happens, get the police."

"Be careful," Heather warned as he moved toward the entrance.

The girls watched tensely as Brian placed his key in the lock. When it clicked open, he cautiously entered the dimly-lit front room. Just as he turned to close the door, however, a deep, angry voice startled him.

"Hold it right there!"

Brian froze in terror as he felt a gun shoved into his back!

# 7

## Vandalism

The armed man frisked Brian, then spun him around. To his astonishment, the college freshman found himself facing a very angry police officer.

"Who are you?" the man demanded.

"Brian Reed, a friend of the Samras," he stuttered.

The cop put his weapon away.

"What, may I ask, are you doing here?" he said gruffly.

"My sister, a friend, and I drove here from Kirby looking for Dr. Samra. We're very close to him. He gave me this key," he added, hoping it would convince the officer of his honesty.

"Where are your accomplices?" the man inquired.

"Outside."

"Go get them," he commanded. "Since you're here, you can help clean up this mess."

He stepped aside, and Brian gasped. Someone had ransacked the house. "What happened?"

"That's what I'm here to figure out," the officer said with a frown.

"I'll get the girls." Brian opened the door to find Heather standing there. Jenn stood timidly several feet away.

"Come in, dear sister," he mocked.

She stepped into the cottage, and Jenn ran up beside her. Then they met the policeman, Sergeant Frank Shade, and heard about Brian's close encounter.

"Your brother could've been shot," the policeman charged.

"We only want to help," Heather defended.

Jenn stood still, afraid to say anything.

"You can," he commented dryly. "This place needs to be cleaned up. I've already made photographs."

"Have you taken fingerprints?" Heather asked.

"I can do my job without your advice, young lady," Officer Shade stormed. "Besides there weren't any. Whoever trashed this place used gloves."

Heather persisted. "What about the footprints outside? One set belongs to you; what about the others?"

"I saw them when I got here an hour ago," the hefty policeman explained. Although Heather's questions were irritating him, Sergeant Shade thought discussing the case aloud might prove beneficial. "It began snowing around midnight," he continued. "The prints looked fresh when I came, so I think the intruder was here not too long ago."

"Would you mind if I take another look?" Brian requested.

"Go ahead," the cop sighed. "But I'm coming with you. You girls take a look in here and tell me if anything's out of the ordinary," he directed.

"Nice guy," Jenn mumbled when the men left. Still, Heather was thrilled to be of assistance.

Outside, Brian examined the two sets of footprints. Sergeant Shade pointed to the smaller pair. "Those are mine. Size ten." His soles had made neat flat marks in the snow while the others contained grooves and were considerably larger.

"Dr. Samra wears about an eight, so the others couldn't be his. I don't think he came here at all."

"At least not since it snowed," Officer Shade added, letting Brian know who was in charge. "The vandal is no doubt a tall man."

Satisfied, they went inside where Heather and Jenn were carefully snooping around.

"Have you found anything?" Sergeant Shade asked.

"We've searched every room, and all we've found is a big mess. Dr. Samra's desk was trashed, especially where he keeps his computer stuff," she added. "I don't know if anything was stolen or not, though. He usually takes everything home at the end of summer."

The policeman considered this for a moment, then said, "Let's put everything back in order."

While the foursome worked, Heather thought about Dr. Morgan: *The argument with Dr. Samra in the hall at Kirby, his tormenting the older professor for information about his latest research, the smooth break-in at Dr. Samra's college office, and the magazine article in* Middle East Today *all pointed to him.*

*But he could only have come here if he didn't have Thursday morning classes,* Heather reasoned silently.

*I'll get Brian to check Morgan's schedule when we go back.*

When they finished, Brian said, "Let's get something to eat. It's past one o'clock."

"That sounds good to me," Jenn agreed. "My stomach's growling."

"How about coming with us, Sergeant Shade?" Heather invited.

"No thanks," he barked. Then his eyes narrowed. "After lunch I want you to head right back to Kirby before you get into more trouble."

"But, how will we help find him?"

The policeman glared at her.

"Time to go Heather!" Brian marched her out to the car with Jenn trailing. Then he drove into town saying "I told you so" every few seconds. "I knew we'd get in hot water."

Jenn kept quiet, determined not to take sides.

They went to a Chinese restaurant, and Heather showed the picture of Dr. Samra to their waiter.

"Have you seen him?" she asked.

But he merely shook his head. As they ate cashew chicken and moo shu pork, the young people discussed whether Dr. Morgan had anything to do with the break-in. They were inclined to think he had, and Brian promised to check the professor's schedule.

After lunch Heather made a bold suggestion. "Let's see if Mr. Greenhowe knows anything." Harry Greenhowe owned a bed-and-breakfast inn and often went deep-sea fishing with the professor.

Brian clapped a hand to his forehead, and Jenn sighed loudly. But somehow Heather convinced them to do it.

"Come in, come in!" Mr. Greenhowe shouted upon seeing the teenagers at his door.

He led them into a sunny parlor where his wife, Lorraine, affectionately greeted the visitors. Then she hurried into the kitchen to make tea, heedless of her company's protests that they'd had enough already.

"I'll bet you're looking for George," the man said, lighting a pipe. "I haven't seen him. And for the life of me, I can't figure the thing out."

Heather was disappointed. The hour-long visit dragged. When they finally stood in the hallway saying their good-byes, a sudden loud sound of screeching tires and crunching metal startled everyone.

Brian looked through the window and cried out, "Someone hit our car!"

The back end of their automobile was buckled like an accordion.

"I'll bet that intruder did it," Heather said through clenched teeth. "We'd better call the police."

"Won't they be thrilled?" Jenn asked Brian.

Mrs. Greenhowe got on the phone while her husband and guests went out to inspect the damage. Heather noticed yellowish paint that had rubbed off from the other vehicle. Then Sergeant Shade and a patrolman arrived.

"I thought I told you to go home," he bellowed.

"We just wanted to visit our friends," Heather said innocently.

They answered some questions while the officers filled out an accident report. Then, feeling dejected, they headed back to Kirby.

"Oh where could Dr. Samra be?" Heather felt frustrated.

"I wish I knew," Brian stated.

While they discussed the case, the trio anxiously checked the side and rearview mirrors every few minutes. At one point, a gray Ford followed them for several miles on the Garden State Parkway. They feared the driver was following them. However, the car finally passed them without incident. When they arrived in their hometown at six o'clock that evening, Heather and Brian dreaded their parents' reaction.

"They are not going to be pleased, I can assure you," Brian worriedly predicted.

"That's for sure." Heather braced for a lecture.

"I'm glad it's not me," Jenn said.

"Thanks a lot," Heather replied.

When Brian pulled up to his house, they noticed several cars, including a police cruiser, in the Samras' driveway.

"I wonder what's going on over there? Let's check it out!" Heather exclaimed.

"Forget it!" Brian said firmly. "First we have to repent of our last set of sins."

As soon as they were out of the car, Jenn hurried off to her house. Brian led the way to the Reeds' back door with Heather trailing behind him. Suddenly the door flew open and nearly startled him out of his wits. Brian was still jumpy from the gun incident.

Mrs. Reed stood there pointing the phone at them. Her face had a worried look. "I've been trying to reach you," she said, her voice tense.

"Mom, did you know the police are at the Samras' again?" Heather broke in.

"That's why I've been trying to call. Miriam phoned a half-hour ago sounding frantic. Their house has been burglarized!"

# 8

# Not Again!

"What a day!" Brian plopped down in a kitchen chair. Heather and Mrs. Reed remained standing.

"Where's Dad?" his sister inquired.

"He's still at work." Their mother regarded them suspiciously. "Okay, what's up?" she asked.

Brian looked at Heather as if to say, "We might as well get this over with."

"Well, you see Mom, Brian, Jenn, and I went to Cape May this morning." The sixteen-year-old braced for the explosion.

"Cape May! Heather, that could've been very dangerous!"

"I know," her daughter murmured.

"Whatever possessed you to do that?" she scolded.

Brian explained, "She had another one of her brainstorms. Jenn and I went to keep her out of trouble."

"I'm going to take away your car." Mrs. Reed's voice was firm.

"It's already been done," Heather said quietly.

"What do you mean?" her mother demanded.

They told her about the wreck. When she was satisfied that no one had been hurt, she announced, "The repair bill will come out of both your pockets."

"Could you drive me back to school tonight?" her son asked.

"Yes, after I make some phone calls," Mrs. Reed said. "I can't believe this!" She shook her head and mumbled as she headed to her office.

When she left, Heather said, "Let's go next door."

"Are you daft?" Brian growled.

"Just nosy," she shrugged.

"And for some dumb reason I try to keep you out of harm's way. Okay, we'll go for a few minutes. But for goodness' sake, don't say anything to Mrs. Samra about the cottage. She's probably already a basket case."

Karen Samra greeted them at the door. She looked tired.

"Is it okay to come in?" Brian asked doubtfully.

"Of course. You're practically family." Karen managed a faint smile. "Mom's in there with two policemen and Dr. Henning. I asked him to come."

The Reverend Arthur Henning had been their minister for many years. Karen lowered her voice. "That FBI agent is in Dad's study. He brought someone with the CIA this time."

"The CIA!" Heather exclaimed.

As Karen led them through the hallway, Heather asked whether anything had been stolen.

"I'm not sure, but the only room they tore up was the study."

*Someone desperately wants something belonging to Dr. Samra. Could it be his manuscript?* Heather thought. "When did the break-in happen?" she asked.

"We're not sure, but it had to be sometime between two-thirty and five this afternoon. That's when Mom and I were out."

*The vandal must have a partner,* Heather considered. *How could the same person go to Cape May and wreck that house, hit our car after lunch, then do this? Timewise it's impossible!* Her thoughts only made her more confused.

"Another strange thing happened today," Karen said, pausing outside the family room. "The bank president called Mom and said Dad withdrew a thousand dollars the morning he disappeared." Tears welled up in her eyes. "One policeman thinks that means Dad ran away. But why would he do such a thing?" Her voice trembled.

Brian put a comforting hand on her shoulder. "I don't think he would."

"Then what happened to him?" she asked helplessly.

For now, no one knew. The three of them entered the family room just as the police officers rose to leave. Karen showed them to the door while Heather and Brian greeted their pastor. Then they took turns hugging Miriam Samra, who fought to maintain her composure. It seemed like a funeral.

Ten minutes later Heather said she and Brian wanted to talk to Agent Roselmann. He wasn't at all surprised to see her and politely shook Brian's hand when she introduced him.

"And this is Mr. Jeremy Ponereau of the Central Intelligence Agency. He's been assigned to this case." He turned to Ponereau. "Heather Reed and her friend, Jenn McLaughlin, were the last to see the professor before his disappearance."

"Please tell me about that," the CIA agent asked Heather.

Mr. Ponereau, like the FBI agent, was a serious-minded professional. But Heather found him better-looking than Mr. Roselmann. His wavy blond hair, green eyes, and deep voice made her heart flutter.

Again she repeated her story. The tall, striking agent listened intently.

"I attended Kirby College," he said when Heather finished. "In fact, I had Dr. Samra for a class."

"Really? Then you know what he's like," she commented. "You know he wouldn't do anything wrong." She paused. "Mr. Roselmann, Karen says because of that large withdrawal from the bank, the police think Dr. Samra may have skipped town. What do you think?"

"That's one theory," he cautioned. "There are other reasons why he may have needed that money."

Brian cleared his throat. "We have a confession to make."

"Oh?" Roselmann raised his eyebrows.

The two teenagers told him about going to Cape May. Heather added, "It was my idea. Jenn and Brian only went to protect me."

"What do you think of the hit-and-run?" Ponereau asked Roselmann.

"Normally, I'd say it was a fluke. But given the current situation, I'm suspicious."

"I would have to second that," Ponereau agreed.

"Did you pick up any clues here?" Heather asked.

"Nothing," Roselmann replied. "This thief knows how to leave a place clean."

Considering the messy condition of the room, the FBI agent's words struck Heather as funny, and she struggled not to laugh. They didn't need another reason to be mad at her! Besides she knew what Mr. Roselmann meant: the intruder had left no fingerprints. Heather could see a pattern developing. *But where does it all lead?* she wondered.

"Mr. Ponereau is now in charge of this case. I expect you to stay out of his way," Roselmann said bluntly. "And another thing," he added, "don't tell Mrs. Samra about Cape May. She has enough on her mind as it is. Leave that to us."

"Of course," Heather agreed. She was grateful for his concern. *Maybe he's human after all,* she thought.

"We could give you a hand cleaning up," Brian offered. "We're getting pretty good at this."

Roselmann clapped his hands. "I'm all for that."

They had been working for twenty minutes when Heather cried out, "Look at this!"

Roselmann rushed to her side. "What is it?"

"I often do secretarial work for Dr. Samra during summer vacation. So I knew to check his file of computer disks." She held up the empty boxes for dramatic effect. "They're gone!"

"Maybe Mrs. Samra was right about Hal Morgan," the FBI agent said grimly. Then he explained Morgan's pursuit of Dr. Samra's book research to Ponereau.

After they completed the clean-up operation, they returned to the family room. Roselmann told Mrs. Samra about the theft. She wasn't surprised. "I still say Hal Morgan is behind this!"

# 9

## Measuring Up Morgan

Heather spent Friday at school mulling over Dr. Samra's disappearance and Hal Morgan's involvement. She had difficulty thinking of anything else. When the dismissal bell finally rang, signaling the start of the weekend, she rushed home to call her brother.

"Did you check Dr. Morgan's schedule?" she asked breathlessly.

"Uh huh. Mrs. Greenberg told me he taught all day yesterday. Because of what's happened he's juggling seven classes." He hesitated. "That doesn't exactly mesh with our theory, does it?"

"No," Heather groaned. "He's too busy to break into houses. And it all seemed so clear last night." She sighed, then silence hung like a curtain between them. "Did you call anyone about the car?" she finally asked.

"Not yet, but I will," he answered. "Before I forget, there's another thing about Horrible Hal. At lunch today Joe told me he needed lots of caffeine to stay awake for his class with Morgan."

"So?"

"To quote him, 'Dr. Morgan is the biggest, most boring flake of a professor I've ever seen.'"

Now the girl was curious. "What did he mean?"

"During their first class, Morgan read straight from notes, which weren't very well organized. Joe also said Morgan didn't sound like any doctor of history to him."

"Then it's too soon to write him off," Heather commented.

"I think so. Anyway I'd better call the garage about the car now. Talk to you later."

Brian's news about Hal Morgan interested Heather, but she couldn't make a connection between it and Dr. Samra's disappearance. She reached into her pet rabbit's cage and pulled her out. As she petted and cuddled the contented Murgatroid, Heather's sharp mind shifted into high gear.

*Dr. Morgan still has a solid alibi—his schedule,* she thought. *Having Dr. Samra away also means much more work for Dr. Morgan. He couldn't possibly have been in Cape May—or have broken into the Samras' house here.* Aloud Heather said, "So, Murgatroid, what do you think?" The rabbit licked her hand in response. "I agree," she remarked, pretending the bunny had offered a comment. "I'll try to contact Mr. Ponereau. Maybe he talked to Dr. Morgan today. I think Mrs. Samra has his number. But I don't want to upset her in any way. I'll call Karen—she probably has it."

Heather put Murgatroid in the cage and within minutes had Jeremy Ponereau on the line. He wasn't pleased.

"What can I do for you?" he asked shortly.

She eagerly told him about the odd way Dr. Morgan had acted in Joe's class. "I was wondering if you found anything out about him? I heard you say last night you planned to visit Kirby today."

"Heather, my work is confidential. You are not part of this search," he retorted.

The cold remark hurt her feelings, and she hung up in disappointment. *If he won't help, I'll just have to find out for myself,* she vowed.

Heather phoned her brother again. "I'd like to find out where Morgan lives," she said.

"Whatever for?" He was clearly annoyed.

"I want to stake out his place to see what he's up to. If he is involved—and I think he is—he may be hiding Dr. Samra in his home."

"That sounds logical," Brian admitted.

"Mrs. Greenberg can give you his address. I checked the phone book, and it's not in there."

"Heather, I have no idea why I let you talk me into these things," he laughed.

"Because we're talking about Dr. Samra's life!" Heather said with conviction.

That did it. Brian gathered enough courage to ask the history department secretary for Hal Morgan's address. He finally took the plunge right before she left for the day.

"Brian, you should know better than to ask for confidential information," she scolded. Then she pulled out a faculty directory and left it open at the right page. She winked slyly at the freshman.

He quickly wrote down "210 Murray Place, Crestwood" and thanked her. On the way back to his dorm, Brian thought, *That rings a bell. Some new condos went up there recently. I know!* He snapped his fingers. *Karen Samra lives there!*

He and Heather had helped her move into the development a year ago. When he called his sister with the news, she could hardly contain herself.

"I'll ask Karen if we can come over tonight. Maybe she lives near him." Then she stopped in mid thought. "Do we still have a car?"

"For now. Eddy Martino said he could fix it next Tuesday."

"Then we can take it tonight!" she exclaimed.

"Heather, Mom said we couldn't use the car, remember?"

"Oh, I forgot!" she groaned. "I've got to think of something." She was pacing her bedroom floor as she talked on the phone. "I know!" she shouted. "Karen is next door. I'll go over and explain our plan. Then I'll ask if we can spend the night. Mom and Dad won't object if she takes me. We can pick you up."

"Okay," Brian agreed. "But don't bring your sidekick." He meant Jenn.

"I thought you liked her," his sister moped.

"That's not the point. I have enough trouble handling you!"

"Well, you don't have to worry because she left after school to spend the weekend with Amy." Jenn's older sister went to college in another state.

When Heather told Karen Samra all that she had learned, the young woman eagerly agreed to her plan.

Then she asked, "Heather, what was Dr. Morgan's address again?"

The sixteen-year-old replied, "It's 210 Murray Place."

"Why that condo is right across from me! Imagine if he's keeping Dad there!" she cried out.

That night from a window seat in Karen's living room, she, Heather, and Brian took turns watching Hal Morgan's home. The professor was there because a light shined in his front room. But there was no sign of other activity after hours of boring observation. To pass the time, Karen made popcorn and put a movie in the VCR.

Well into the night when Heather was about to let Brian take over for her, she noticed some movement at Morgan's front door.

"What is it?" Brian asked, moving cautiously toward the window.

"Dr. Morgan just came out and got into a red car," Heather replied.

"That's funny," Karen frowned. "He drives a black one."

"This one's red," Heather repeated. "But a black car is there too. He left the light on in the house. Maybe he has company," she concluded. Neither vehicle matched the description of the one that struck their car in Cape May.

Heather moved to the couch as Brian took her place at the window.

Fifteen minutes later a strange thing happened. The light in Morgan's front room suddenly went out! But the professor hadn't returned.

"He must've had company, and they went to bed," Brian pondered out loud. "I wonder. . ."

But he stopped in mid sentence when he saw Hal Morgan himself leave the condominium and get into the black car!

# 10

# Stakeout

W hat is it?" Heather pleaded.

"If that isn't the strangest thing!"

"What? What!" She was beside herself.

"Morgan left the house awhile ago, right?" he asked.

"Right."

"Well, not two minutes ago he drove off in that black car." Brian scratched his chin.

"Are you sure it was him?" Karen asked innocently.

"I know who he is," he said trying not to sound annoyed. "But how did he return without our seeing him?"

"I don't know," Karen said. "Each of these units has only one entrance."

He thought hard. "We haven't taken our eyes off that place since we got here. So how did he go back inside without our seeing him, and what happened to that red car?"

"Maybe he's been in there all along," Heather said, suddenly looking quite pleased with herself.

Now her brother became openly irritated. "Don't mess around, Heather. This is confusing enough!"

"Maybe Morgan never left," she smiled knowingly.

"But that doesn't make sense," Karen objected. "We saw him go."

"Maybe not. What if the first guy wasn't Hal Morgan?" she persisted.

Karen looked bewildered. "Do you mean we saw someone who only looked like him?"

"Ah!" Brian smiled slyly. "So Morgan has a twin!"

"Exactly!" Heather exclaimed.

"A twin?" Karen slowly caught on.

"Now it all seems to fit." Heather nodded to herself.

Brian understood too. "My roommate told me Dr. Morgan's been acting weirder than usual in class. He doesn't know what he's talking about and is disorganized. Well, that isn't the same guy I had last semester. Though Hal Morgan may be a twit, he knows his stuff. Anyway I'll bet his twin taught Joe's class the other day."

"Hey! Remember those footprints in the snow at Cape May?" Heather shouted. "What size did you say they were?"

"They could easily match a man of his size," he said excitedly.

"What's this about Cape May?" Karen asked.

Brian and Heather gave each other a look that meant, "Go ahead and tell her."

"You're amazing!" their friend said when Heather finished the story.

"But please don't mention anything to your mother," Brian cautioned.

"The agents didn't tell her because she was already too worked up," Heather explained.

"Did you say nothing was stolen?" Karen asked.

"That's right," Heather replied.

"The vandals want something pretty badly. It must have been those computer disks they took from the house." Then Karen's lip quivered, and she began to cry. "Where is my father? What if he did get in with the wrong people on his trip?" she added fearfully.

Heather put an arm around her shoulders. Brian's eyes welled up with tears.

"I understand where you're coming from," Brian soothed, "but we have no good reason not to trust him."

"He's right," Heather agreed. "But you go ahead and cry. This is really hard on you." After some minutes she suggested, "Let's tell Mr. Ponereau about our discovery." The teenager checked her watch; it was eleven-thirty. "I hope he's a night owl."

He wasn't. When Heather called him, Ponereau sounded groggy. "Who is this?" he mumbled.

"It's Heather Reed. I'm sorry I woke you up."

After a pause he asked impatiently, "What is it?"

"I have major news about Hal Morgan," she said.

"At this hour? Oh, go on," he sighed.

The teenager told him the entire story beginning with Joe Rutli's observation about the professor. "Could you come over and check this out for yourself?" she concluded.

"I guess so," he said. He took directions and promised to get there as soon as he could. Fifteen minutes later he

arrived looking unbelievably fresh, especially considering how sleepy he had sounded on the phone.

*Not a hair out of place,* Heather thought with a smile.
*Mr. Cool. Even though he was rude to me earlier, he's still
cute.*

First Ponereau requested that they turn off all the
lights. He wanted the house to look as if Karen had gone
to bed. Then using high-powered binoculars, he kept
watch at the window seat.

By one o'clock, the others were getting silly. They
began teasing each other about their childhood pranks,
especially Heather's. Ponereau paid no attention. In-
stead he fixed a steady eye on the Morgan condo.

Suddenly he interrupted their hushed laughter. "I see
some activity."

Heather jumped up and rushed to his side.

"Take it easy!" Ponereau commanded.

Brian and Karen remained on the couch since there
wasn't room for everyone at the window.

Heather noticed that both the red and black cars had
just pulled up in front of Morgan's place. When the men
climbed out of the vehicles, Ponereau muttered, "They're
twins all right."

They watched the shadowy figures move through the
darkness toward the door.

"Look!" Heather exclaimed. "One of them is carrying
something."

Ponereau zeroed in on the object.

"Can you tell what it is?" she pleaded.

He laughed sarcastically. "Something from the convenience store."

Impatience got the best of the teenager. "Can't you just go over and demand to know what they've been doing?" she cried out. "What if Dr. Samra's there?"

Although Heather knew that wasn't likely, she was anxious for something to happen.

Ponereau regarded her curiously. Heather had difficulty interpreting the look. Finally he said, "I seriously doubt they're holding him hostage over there. Not that it's impossible, but . . ."

"Why couldn't they?" Heather challenged, her eyes flashing.

"Okay, so I don't know for sure!" Ponereau admitted in frustration. "But all we can do is wait and watch."

The severe look he gave her made Heather think twice about confronting him further. She fell into a moody silence.

When the Morgan brothers entered the condo, a light went on downstairs. A few minutes later, it went off again. It seemed as though they had gone to bed. But Ponereau wasn't counting on it.

"I'd like to keep an eye on them just the same," he announced.

"Do you mind if I go to bed?" Karen yawned sleepily.

"No, I don't." Ponereau relaxed for a minute. "In fact, the rest of you can if you want to."

Heather didn't want to miss anything, so she stretched out on the living room couch. Brian slept nearby in a sleeping bag. But there was nothing else to miss since no further activity occurred that night.

By six o'clock Saturday morning, everyone in Karen Samra's house was awake. Heather was amused at Jeremy Ponereau's appearance. "Mr. Cool" now had dark circles under his eyes and bearded stubble on his face. And he had more than a few hairs out of place!

Heather headed to the kitchen to help Karen with breakfast.

A little while later, the group sat down to ham, eggs, and French toast. Then they mapped out a strategy for the day. Ponereau thought they should keep a close watch on the Morgans all weekend.

"You're welcome to stay here." Karen sounded somewhat uneasy, but she wanted to help find her missing father. Then she remembered something. "The condo under mine is empty. Maybe you could arrange to rent it for a few days."

"That's a good idea," Ponereau agreed. He quickly called the landlord, who agreed to let him use the first floor unit. Although Brian needed to get back to campus, Heather remained with Karen until Sunday morning.

Ponereau watched the Morgans again Saturday night. But when the girls checked with him Sunday morning, he hadn't discovered any further information. Heather tried to cheer Karen up as they drove to church.

"At least we know Hal Morgan is up to no good," Heather encouraged. "We are making progress."

But even she was troubled by what they still didn't know. Had the Morgan brothers broken into Dr. Samra's college office and his homes? Were they keeping the professor as a prisoner? If not, where was he?

On Monday morning Jenn breathlessly caught up with Heather as she walked to school.

"Where've you been?" Heather asked. "I thought you were coming home last night."

"We planned on it, but Amy came down with the flu. My parents didn't want to leave her."

"How is she?" Heather asked in concern.

"Better this morning. But I'm a wreck from wondering what I've missed!"

Heather brought her up to date on the weekend's events.

"Oh, I wish we didn't have school today," Jenn complained.

"I know exactly what you mean," her petite friend agreed. "How will we think of anything else?"

When school ended several hours later, the girls visited the professor's wife to see how she was doing. Shortly after they arrived the doorbell rang. Heather eagerly ran to answer it. Both Ponereau and Roselmann stood there looking very serious when she opened the door.

"What's wrong?" she asked fearfully.

"We'll tell you when we see Mrs. Samra," Roselmann answered calmly.

Heather hurried them into the kitchen where the professor's wife was cooking dinner. The older woman caught her breath at the sight of their faces.

"We have news," Ponereau announced gravely.

# 11

## Catching a Thief

D id you find my husband?" Mrs. Samra asked with an eerie calmness.

"No," Ponereau responded quickly, "but a Kirby policeman found out Hal Morgan's brother Henry has a drunken driving record. He's also been arrested several times for petty theft and assault with a deadly weapon."

"Is that the big news?" Heather asked disappointedly. A glance at Jenn told her she too wondered what was the big deal.

Ponereau gave the teenager a sideways look, then continued. "The history department chairman did some homework and discovered Dr. Morgan lied on his résumé about his employment record. He has never stayed in one place more than a year."

"So they *are* guilty!" Heather shouted.

"What have they done to my husband?" Mrs. Samra demanded. "That is the only thing that matters to me. I don't care what kind of background the Morgans have."

"We're investigating to see if they have him," Roselmann told her.

"I wonder whether Morgan has classes this afternoon?" Ponereau asked out of the blue.

"Probably," Heather said. "He's teaching seven of them, so chances are he's there. I'll call the History Department," she offered, glad to be of help. In a few minutes she announced, "He had three this morning and one more at four-thirty."

"Good." Ponereau's green eyes took on an intense look. Then he mumbled, "They'd be meeting in Foster Hall. I can find the room easily enough." He cleared his throat. "I think it's time to make an arrest."

"How will you know which Morgan is in the class?" Jenn questioned.

"You said one of them was poorly prepared and disorganized, right?" he asked Heather.

"Uh huh."

"That shouldn't be too hard then," he said vaguely. He faced Roselmann. "I'll take a police officer with me, Pete. Maybe you should stay near the condo in case they plan a get-away."

"Sounds good," the FBI man agreed.

"Just find my husband," Mrs. Samra ordered as the men left her house.

Heather and Jenn longed to go with Ponereau, but they knew he wouldn't let them. So they stayed with Mrs. Samra and waited as the day stretched into evening. At seven-thirty Police Chief Cullen stopped by looking excited.

"What has happened, Andy?" Mrs. Samra begged.

The large man joined them in the family room. In excited tones he described what had happened after the CIA agent picked him up at the station and took him to the college.

"When we neared Morgan's classroom, Ponereau grabbed a male student as he headed inside."

"What did he do to him?" Jenn asked.

"I'm getting there, I'm getting there," Chief Cullen protested. "He asked the fellow if he noticed anything different about his professor from one class to the next."

"Did he?" Jenn's eyes sparkled.

"He sure did! He said one day the prof was bright and informed, the next as stupid as a squirrel crossing a highway."

"Then what?" Heather prodded.

"Ponereau told the student to ask as many questions as he could. Well, the kid obeyed, and Morgan got so worked up by the fourth time that he stormed out of the room."

"Did you catch him?" Mrs. Samra asked.

"Yes, ma'am. We took him to the station and questioned him for forty-five minutes."

"And?" Heather leaned forward eagerly.

"We have him in the slammer," he smiled.

"Obviously he was the fake professor," the girl commented. "What about his brother?"

"Roselmann arrested him at the condo for theft."

"What did he steal?" She felt her heart race.

Unfortunately the ringing phone interrupted them. They waited as Mrs. Samra answered it.

"Yes, of course," they heard her say. Then she addressed her young neighbor. "Heather, Mr. Ponereau wants to speak with you."

The teenager was puzzled. "What for?"

"He didn't tell me," Mrs. Samra shrugged.

"I thought he might be calling," Chief Cullen said smugly. He leaned back and hooked his fingers through his belt loops.

"Hello, Mr. Ponereau, this is Heather. Is that right? I'd be happy to try. Yes, I have a computer. What about Dr. Samra? Oh. Okay. I'll see you there. Bye."

The excited teenager could hardly contain herself. "He said Hal Morgan had all Dr. Samra's computer disks at the condo. And one had his new book on it."

"That's what he stole," added the policeman.

"I knew it! I just knew it," Mrs. Samra exclaimed. Then she asked restlessly, "Did they find George?"

"He wasn't at their condo," Heather said, but quickly added, "Mr. Ponereau says at the very beginning of one computer file there's some text in a foreign language. Plus, he can't get into the rest of it without a special code. Since I've assisted Dr. Samra the past few summers, Mr. Ponereau thinks I could get into it. And then we just might solve this mystery!"

## 12

# Unexpected Villain

Agent Ponereau arrived at the Reeds' by eight-thirty. He accompanied Heather to her father's study where the family kept their computer. Her parents struggled to stay out of the way and sat anxiously in the family room with Mrs. Samra and Jenn. Chief Cullen had gone back to the station to fill out a report.

"Heather, I have something to tell you before you try to get into this file," Ponereau said soberly. "I found some important information on another disk." He looked grim.

"You did? That's great—isn't it?" She could tell something troubled him.

"Probably not for you or anyone close to Dr. Samra," he warned.

"What do you mean?" Her face went pale.

"The thing is full of top secret information," he charged. "Only the master terrorists have access to stuff like that."

"You're wrong!" she cried out.

He attempted to get her back on track. "Look, Heather, as I told you over the phone, I can't get into part of the disk. If possible, I want you to get into it. At the beginning of the file there's something in another language." Suddenly he got irritated. "Heather, are you listening?"

"Yes," she sighed heavily. "I'll see what I can do. But you're wrong about Dr. Samra!" She looked him straight in the eyes.

Ponereau ignored the comment and placed the disk in the computer. He brought up just a single line. "Can you make any sense out of that?" the agent asked.

Heather recognized the language immediately. "Uh huh. It's Greek."

"Greek?" he asked in surprise.

"Yes, Greek," she responded. "Dr. Samra reads and speaks it fluently. I sure don't." Ponereau frowned, and Heather continued. "I'll bet there's something in this part that will prove Dr. Samra did nothing wrong." Her voice was filled with determination.

"Look, Heather, we know now what the Morgans were after. They had nothing to do with his kidnapping. Dr. Samra is looking more and more guilty of wrong-doing."

"Maybe the Morgans knew more than they were telling," she suggested. "How do you know they didn't kill him?" Heather shuddered involuntarily at the terrible thought.

"I doubt that," he said coolly.

"Well, they must know what happened to Dr. Samra! Didn't they have anything to do with his disappearance?" She tossed her long hair defiantly.

"No, they didn't," Ponereau said evenly. "They're losers. One is a poor excuse for a professor. The other is a second-rate con artist. They wanted to get rich and famous off Dr. Samra's new book. That's all there was to it. So you may have to change your mind about your friend, Heather. The Morgan brothers simply took advantage of the situation like looters after a hurricane."

She became touchy. "I know Dr. Samra better than that, Mr. Ponereau."

"I'm sure you don't want to think evil of him, but we have to look at the cold, hard facts." His piercing eyes narrowed.

"They're cold and hard all right," she muttered. Then Heather thought about something else. "By the way, did the Morgans smash into our car at Cape May?"

"No. That was done by a careless cab driver."

"What about the break-ins?" she challenged.

Now it was Ponereau's turn to get jumpy. "The Morgans were behind those because they wanted that manuscript. Now, Heather, do you think we could get back to this Greek thing? I must get this translated."

"I have an idea. Our youth pastor at church knows Greek. I could call and ask him to come over."

Ponereau rolled his eyes. "How long would that take?"

"He lives in town, so it shouldn't take much time at all," she predicted.

Before the agent could say yes or no, Heather was on the phone calling Dick Walker. Unfortunately, she only got his answering machine. At the sound of the beep, she said, "Dick, this is Heather Reed. Please call me as soon as you get in. It's very important. My number is 555-1322. Thanks!"

"That's just great!" Ponereau was angry now. "This could take hours, and I'm supposed to get together with Pete Roselmann at nine-fifteen. He doesn't know anything about this Greek message yet, and I can't afford to waste time."

"I don't know any other way to do this," she defended. Then she had a brainstorm. "Hey, wait a minute!" She snapped her fingers. "My minister can!"

The agent groaned. "You've already let another person in on the case, and I can't afford security leaks. You don't know what could be at stake." He paused. "Now that you've already called this, uh, youth pastor, let's just stay with him."

"Don't worry. Dick will come through."

"I suppose that's the best I can do for now," he sighed. "Meanwhile, I'd like you to try and get into the rest of the file. Do you think you can?"

"I can sure try. When I worked for Dr. Samra last summer, he had me use a few access codes."

"Try them all," Ponereau demanded. "I have to know what's in there." He consulted his watch. "I'll be going. You keep working. And if you do get into that file, wait for me before you do another thing. I should be back by ten."

The teenager nodded, then stopped abruptly when he added, "Don't let another soul near that computer."

"What if Dick gets here first?" she inquired.

"Dick?" he questioned.

"You know, my youth pastor. The one who knows Greek."

"Ask him if he understands the message!" he sputtered. Ponereau threw his hands up in the air and stomped out of the room.

"Boy, is he in a rotten mood tonight!" Heather grumbled. Then she went to the family room and told them in general terms what had happened.

"He actually thinks Dr. Samra is the bad guy in this!" she exclaimed. "Can you believe that? I mean, how incredible!"

Mrs. Samra's shoulders drooped. She looked tired and stressed.

"I certainly do not agree with him," her mother stated, trying to encourage her older friend. "The very idea!"

"Well, I don't either," Mr. Reed chimed in. "He's the most decent man I've ever known. We need to remember that no matter what anyone else says."

Jenn hugged Mrs. Samra.

Heather hurried back to the study with its computer challenge. "I'll clear his good name," she announced to the walls.

She put her honey-brown hair up in a pony tail, then set to work. The first thing Heather did was gaze at the message in Greek out of curiosity.

"You look like you mean business," Jenn said, poking her head in the door.

"I sure do," she nodded, forgetting Ponereau's warning not to let anyone else near the computer.

Jenn leaned over her friend's shoulder as Heather remembered the codes Dr. Samra had instructed her to use. To her amazement, the first one worked! "Jenn, look at this!"

But then the phone interrupted them.

"Heather!" her mother called. "It's Dick."

"What awful timing!" she moaned, not wanting to leave her work. Then she realized how much she needed Dick's help and quickly picked up the phone on the desk. Heather told him why she had to see him as soon as possible, and he promised to come right over.

"So you got into the program," Jenn said triumphantly. "Now we wait for Dick, right?"

"Wrong." Again she ignored Ponereau's charge and started reading. And the more Heather saw, the more excited she became. "Jenn, this is part of Dr. Samra's new book!" she exclaimed.

"Wow!"

Then just as suddenly she frowned. "But there's something wrong here. Look at this information."

Jenn peered at the screen and didn't like what she saw. "It's as if he worked with terrorists," she commented darkly.

"Uh huh. But Ponereau's still wrong," Heather insisted. "Dr. Samra must've come by this honestly." She refused to think evil of her old friend.

"I hope so." Jenn didn't seem so sure.

A knock at the door brought them to attention. Heather scrambled to call up the original file in case it was Ponereau. When the door opened, sandy-haired Dick Walker stood there.

"Dick," she said breathlessly, "please come in."

"Hi, girls. What gives?" The twenty-three-year-old pulled up a chair in the small study.

Heather showed him the Greek message.

Although Dick had no difficulty translating it, the contents took him by surprise. "This is from the Lord's Prayer in Matthew," he said. "In English, it means 'deliver us from evil.' The word *evil* appears in capital letters. That's an unusual way to write it," he explained. "For whatever it's worth, though, the Greek for evil is pronounced PON-ER-OO."

# 13

## Deliver Us from Evil

The phrase "deliver us from evil" played like a broken record in Heather's head. *Evil . . . Pon-er-oo . . . PONEREAU! Oh no!* she thought. *What if he's not really with the CIA? Is Mr. Roselmann okay? What if Agent Ponereau kidnapped Dr. Samra and killed him? What if he tries to kill me?*

Jenn was also incredulous. "Can you believe this?"

"Believe what?" Dick asked puzzled.

"The CIA agent's last name is Ponereau," Heather explained dramatically.

"Oh boy." Dick ran a hand over his forehead.

"And to think I liked him!" Jenn looked shaken. "What do we do now?"

Heather felt stunned and angry. "Now that we know the truth, I wonder what Dr. Samra would want me to do," she considered. "One thing's for sure—Mr. Ponereau can't find out that we know about him."

Dick Walker looked thoughtful. "You're in a tough position. Whatever you do, be very careful."

"For now I'm going to copy out this whole file before Ponereau gets back," Heather stated, turning on the printer. "Maybe Dr. Samra left other messages for me."

"What will you tell Mr. Ponereau?" Jenn fretted.

"I'm not sure yet," Heather frowned. "One step at a time."

"Well, I'd better get out of here before he comes back," the redhead announced. "I'll be with your folks."

Fifteen minutes later Heather finished the printout. She was slipping it in a desk drawer just as she heard the doorbell. When Ponereau walked into the study, she tried to act as normally as possible.

"Is this the Greek genius?" he asked.

"Of sorts," Dick said, trying to sound friendly. "I'm Dick Walker."

"Jeremy Ponereau," the agent said, absently shaking Dick's outstretched hand. "So, what did the message say?" he demanded, leaning over the computer.

"You can't believe how disappointing this is," Heather sighed. "Dick says it was only the Lord's Prayer."

"The Lord's Prayer?" Ponereau's face went blank. "That's crazy! What did Dr. Samra mean by that?"

The pretty teenager crossed her arms and shrugged.

"Did you access the rest of the program?" he questioned hopefully.

"Uh huh."

His green eyes narrowed. "You didn't read it, did you?"

"You told me not to," Heather stated.

"So he did use a password," the agent said. "What was it?"

Heather told him, "It's A-S-L-A-N."

"May I ask what that means?" Ponereau barked.

"It's a character from a book," she explained. Out of the corner of her eye Heather saw Dick smile. "He likes the story and uses the code quite often," she explained truthfully.

Ponereau seemed satisfied with the explanation. "Now we're getting somewhere. I'll take that disk now."

She exited from the document and handed the disk to him. The agent stared at her suspiciously.

"Is something wrong?" she asked.

"I was just wondering why the professor used that particular Greek passage."

The teenager did her best to look innocent. "It does seem strange, doesn't it?" she asked.

He shoved the disk into his breast pocket. "I must get going. Nice meeting you," he said to Dick without really meaning it. "I appreciate the assistance."

For a moment everything about him seemed normal, as if Dr. Samra had sent the wrong message. *But that's not so*, Heather reminded herself.

"What will you do next?" her dad asked the agent as they said good-bye at the door. Mr. Reed was flanked by his wife, Jenn, Mrs. Samra, Dick, and Heather.

"Step up the search for Dr. Samra. I have a strong hunch he's hip-deep in trouble."

"I happen to think you're wrong," Mrs. Reed boldly interrupted.

"As they say, everyone is entitled to his—or her — opinion. Besides you have a built-in bias."

Heather got really angry. *Oh, I'd like to punch his lights out!* she thought. But she kept quiet until he walked out the door. Then she let out a frustrated yell when the group returned to the family room.

"Heather, whatever are you howling about?" her father asked.

"Jeremy Ponereau is a crook!" she charged.

"What?" her parents and Mrs. Samra said together. They wore shocked expressions.

"Heather, that's a serious charge. Are you certain?" her father asked.

"I'm afraid she's right," Dick defended her. Then he told them about the Greek message.

No one said anything for a few minutes as the news sank in.

"I'm so proud of you," her mother hugged her. Everyone else agreed the sixteen-year-old had done well.

"This is very serious," Mr. Reed then remarked. "I think we should tell Peter Roselmann and Chief Cullen right away."

Heather had reached the same conclusion. Never one to delay, she called the Kirby Police station. "Chief Cullen, this is Heather Reed," she began. "I'm at home, and Mrs. Samra's here too. We have to talk to you and Mr. Roselmann as soon as possible. It's super serious!"

# 14

## On the Scent

When Heather hung up, she ran to get the computer printout. She vowed to all present, "I'm going to comb through this until I find out exactly what's going on." As her eyes sped over the document, its contents further shocked her. Dr. Samra had recorded pages and pages of explosive information about terrorists for his new book.

"I'll bet this is what the Morgans were after," Mrs. Samra commented.

"Look," Heather pointed out in dismay. "He admits terrorist leaders told him this stuff."

"Heather, you don't think . . ." Jenn stammered. She couldn't bring herself to say what was on her mind.

The others also shuddered to think Dr. Samra might have been involved with international thugs.

"I suppose he had to meet with them as part of his research," Dick said uncertainly.

"I won't let myself believe Dr. Samra's a terrorist," Jenn blurted, her mood suddenly changed. "He'd never do something like that." She lifted her chin defiantly.

Again Heather explored the printout. Several minutes later she yelled, "Look at this!"

They all drew closer. "What is it?" her mother asked.

"This proves he's okay, even if it is a little confusing." Heather read aloud a baffling message: "*'Tuesday, January 10, Director, CIA in Valley Forge. Council for Democracy. Critical conference on Middle East terrorism. Stop Matthew 6:13!'*" She added, "That's tomorrow!"

"There's the Lord's Prayer again!" Dick exclaimed.

"It's another warning about Jeremy Ponereau," Jenn stated.

In the few minutes before the officers arrived, Heather looked harder for further leads. Nothing was forthcoming. "I think that's it," she remarked. "I wish he'd told us what to do."

"Perhaps he already did," said the professor's wife. When Heather lifted an eyebrow, she continued. "I think he wants you to report that awful Ponereau person."

"I agree," Jenn nodded decisively.

"I just hope he's all right, and we're not too late," the teenager murmured.

The sound of the doorbell interrupted them. Heather rushed to answer it, then led Peter Roselmann and Chief Cullen to the family room. The men looked perplexed, wondering why they had been summoned.

"What's going on?" the FBI agent asked after introductions had been made and everyone was seated.

"We have shocking news," Heather said. Then she explained the CIA agent's request that she get into Dr. Samra's program.

"Why you?" Roselmann asked.

"Because I've done secretarial work for Dr. Samra," she reminded him.

"So you did access it!" Chief Cullen said proudly.

"Uh huh. But right before that part, Mr. Ponereau showed me a message in Greek. Since neither of us knew the language, I called Dick, and he translated the words. The English is *deliver us from EVIL*."

"And what else did you find?" Roselmann was literally on the edge of his seat.

"Lots of scary stuff about terrorism, for one thing," she began.

"It's really amazing," Jenn added.

Roselmann pleaded, "Go on. Go on, Heather."

She took a deep breath. "First let me tell you what Dick says about the Greek message. The Greek word for *evil* is pronounced PON-ER-OO, and Dr. Samra highlighted it by writing it in capital letters."

"Holy cow," Chief Cullen whistled. "Do you still have the disk?"

"No, but I made a printout," she said.

"Good girl!" he praised.

"There's more." Heather repeated the message concerning the CIA Director and the Council for Democracy.

"I think George wanted us to find out Jeremy Ponereau is evil before it's too late," Mrs. Reed offered.

Roselmann and Chief Cullen each examined the printout as the others looked on silently.

"Does Ponereau know about your discovery?" the tall FBI agent asked anxiously.

"Not yet," Heather replied.

"We told him what the Lord's Prayer meant without mentioning the clue about his name," Dick added.

"Heather, you've performed quite a service for us," Chief Cullen complimented her. "I'd say this clears Dr. Samra of any wrongdoing."

The relieved teenager thanked him humbly. Then she asked, "Do you think Jeremy Ponereau really is with the CIA?"

Roselmann nodded. "Yes. I've known him for several years." He pursed his lips and said, "It looks like Dr. Samra is innocent, but I'm troubled that he knows all that information about terrorists. How in the world did he get that?"

"Beats me," Chief Cullen remarked, sucking his teeth.

"And where in the world is he?" asked a worried Mrs. Samra.

"I wish I knew. The Morgans didn't have him, and there's been no ransom note," Roselmann said.

Heather worked on a different angle. "I wonder if Mr. Ponereau is working alone?"

"Me too," Chief Cullen said. "Pete, I think we'll need reinforcements." When his colleague agreed, the officer got on the phone. At eleven-thirty three other police officers arrived. One of them was a young woman named Amy Weaver. Nick Holmes, a handsome black man, appeared very professional. And Mike Armgard, dark-haired and unshaven, looked the toughest.

Andrew Cullen introduced everyone. Then they listened to the fantastic story Heather had uncovered.

"I'll take the printout," Roselmann said. "I want to look at it more closely, but I don't have much time now. Can you remember anything else you want to tell us?" he asked Heather.

"Not right now," she admitted.

"Then I'd like to see a phone book," Roselmann requested.

Heather's father produced one immediately, and the agent looked up the Council for Democracy's number. He dialed it and asked for information about the CIA Director's visit and conference Dr. Samra wrote about. Then he hung up. "There is going to be a meeting, and it's scheduled for nine o'clock tomorrow morning."

"That's right!" Mr. Reed snapped his fingers. "I got a press release about it several days ago."

"I'd like to arrange some police protection for all of you until this situation gets resolved," Chief Cullen stated. "When Ponereau reads that document, then realizes Heather might have taken a look, well . . ."

His frankness sent a chill through the small group.

"We'll also need to keep an eye on Ponereau tonight," Chief Cullen proceeded. "He's staying in a King of Prussia motel."

"What should we do?" Mrs. Reed asked nervously.

The stout police chief advised, "Lay low as much as possible until this passes. I'll have a constant patrol watching this and the Samras' house. Dick and Jenn, I think you folks are safe enough."

"I wonder how my husband knows about Ponereau?" Mrs. Samra asked tensely, a far-away look in her eyes. "And where could he be? I hope he's just hiding somewhere where Ponereau can't find him."

"Me too," Cullen agreed. "Well, let's get a move on," he told his crew. "We'll keep you posted," he promised the rest. Then the five law-enforcement officials left.

"I think you should spend the night with us," Mrs. Reed suggested to Miriam Samra.

"I'd like to, but what if it looks suspicious?" she questioned.

"We can walk over at your normal bedtime," Mr. Reed offered. "Then I'll sneak you out through the back door. I think we'd all feel better if you stayed here."

"I'm nervous," Jenn remarked.

"We probably should tell your parents," Mr. Reed stated. "But we can't say too much."

"Can she stay too?" Heather pleaded.

"I don't think so," her mother said. "That might be stretching it if someone is watching."

"That makes sense," Jenn said. "I'll go over now just like I usually do."

"Not alone, you won't," Dick objected. "I'll walk you home."

"And I'll call your parents right now," Heather's dad said.

At midnight the Reed household began to calm down. Just then the phone rang, and Mrs. Reed answered it. It was the CIA agent.

"It's very late, Mr. Ponereau," she said, trying to sound calm. "All right, we'll see you in a few minutes." She looked a little frightened as she faced the curious group. "He wants to talk with you Miriam."

"Whatever for?" Mrs. Samra asked.

"He wants to question you again," she said simply.

"That's strange," Heather observed. "How did he know she was still here?"

"He tried reaching her at home," Elaine Reed explained.

"I want Andy Cullen to know about this," her husband said.

The police chief told Mr. Reed that Ponereau might be testing them all to see if they knew more than they were saying. "Whatever he's got planned for that meeting tomorrow, he needs to make sure there are no last minute twists. We'll make sure you're well covered, but he'll never know we're there. All right?"

"Of course," Patrick Reed said. "We'll do our best." He hung up and reported the chief's end of the conversation. "Let's just keep our wits about us—and pray for wisdom."

"Do you think he'll get violent?" his daughter asked, wide-eyed.

"Oh, Heather!" Mrs. Reed scolded.

Her father refereed. "I wouldn't worry about that. At this point, he can't afford to have anything go wrong. Besides we have police watching us."

"Oh, if only this mystery were solved!" Mrs. Samra exclaimed.

Jeremy Ponereau arrived shortly. He exchanged greetings with Heather, her parents, and Mrs. Samra.

"I'd really like to wrap things up as soon as possible," the CIA agent tried to be pleasant. "Mrs. Samra, is there anything further you can tell me since we last spoke?" Ponereau leaned forward hoping to harvest some new fruit of his labor.

Miriam Samra ran a thin hand through her tousled hair. "I've told you everything I know."

His mood shifted. "Your husband's manuscript disk contains some highly sensitive information," Ponereau said grimly. "He obviously cooperated with terrorists to get it."

Heather waited tensely for her reaction.

"No matter what you say, Mr. Ponereau, I trust George completely," she retorted.

Now he tried intimidation. "He got a big advance for that new book of his. Why wouldn't he go to fantastic lengths to make it a bestseller?"

"You are a most offensive young man," she stormed. One eyelid twitched with emotion.

"I'm only searching for the truth," he defended, raising his hands in mock surrender.

"I'll bet you are!" she raged.

*Don't give us away,* Heather inwardly pleaded. *If you do, we'll all be in big trouble!*

Her parents were thinking along the same line. They too held their breath in the charged atmosphere.

"I resent your foolish accusations," Miriam Samra huffed.

"Now, now, it's very late, and we're all a little testy over this," Mr. Reed said, trying to calm her down.

Ponereau ignored him. "I don't really care that you don't like me, Mrs. Samra. My evidence is what matters. It tells me George Samra is an enemy of the state, and I have every intention of finding him— unless, of course, terrorists already have." Then his green eyes narrowed into knifelike slits. "I can't even be totally sure you don't know things you shouldn't."

"How dare you!" Mrs. Samra shouted angrily. Her hands trembled.

"I'll tell you," he said in his cool, even way, "your husband has been working with terrorists. His Lebanese background doesn't exactly delight me at this point either. Who knows what kind of connections he's made? Or what he's told any of you?" His eyes swept around the room. "I'd be very careful."

The tone of his voice frightened Heather. He was plainly warning them.

Mrs. Reed rose from her chair in a composed manner and addressed Agent Ponereau. She had remained silent, but now her words carried unquestioning authority. "Get out of this house."

"Very well." Ponereau got up. "Thank you for your time," he said calmly. Then he showed himself to the door.

Heather reached across the couch where she and Mrs. Samra were sitting and took the older woman's shaking hands.

"I never want to go through anything like that again!" the professor's wife sobbed. "What a nightmare this has been!"

Mr. Reed telephoned Chief Cullen. "My people saw Ponereau leave in a huff. What happened?" the policeman asked.

"He thinks Dr. Samra is in cahoots with terrorists. Called him an enemy of the state," repeated Heather's father. "After he got really offensive, my wife tossed him out!"

"I hope you handled yourselves well," Chief Cullen said anxiously.

"Quite well, considering."

"Do you think he suspected anything?" the police chief asked.

"I don't know," Patrick Reed stated.

"Mrs. Samra probably should stay with you tonight. It's been a bad time for her."

"We've already arranged that." Then Mr. Reed told him what he'd done with Jenn and how much her parents knew.

"That's fine," Andrew Cullen said. "Talk to you soon."

"I think we're all exhausted and should get to bed," Mrs. Reed suggested. "Come on, Miriam. Heather and I will get you settled in the guest room."

In a few minutes, the older woman was ready for bed. But tears filled her eyes. "I have this terrible feeling. What if George. . ."

"We have to give him the benefit of the doubt," Heather reassured her. "And who would you believe first—him, or that Ponereau creature?"

Traces of a smile crossed the woman's trembling lips. "Thanks, Honey."

Then the sound of Mr. Reed's urgent voice interrupted them. "Ladies," he called. "Please come down here right away."

They looked at each other in alarm and hurried to the first floor.

Officer Amy Weaver stood in the foyer next to Heather's father. "I know it's horribly late, but Chief Cullen has asked me to escort you to the police station right away."

"What for?" Heather asked.

"I'm afraid I can't tell you," she stated.

"Give me a few minutes to get dressed," Mrs. Samra said and rushed back to the guest room to change again.

Ten minutes later, Officer Weaver rushed all of them to the station. Peter Roselmann met them at the door and escorted them down a long hall to a private back room. When Heather stepped inside, she screamed, "Dr. Samra!"

# 16

## Startling News

Heather flew into the professor's arms, and he nearly smothered her in a happy embrace. Then he eagerly reached for his wife. They lingered for a few minutes, then he hugged Heather's parents.

Chief Cullen sat perched on a desk near Mike Armgard. Peter Roselmann took charge, signaling for everyone to be seated.

"We all have questions, so let's get started," he said. "After we left you, Dr. Samra called from the airport. We sent a detail to pick him up."

Heather interrupted. "Where have you been?"

Dr. Samra glanced at Roselmann, who nodded his approval. "I've been with an old college friend in Michigan."

"So you weren't kidnapped?" she remarked.

"No, I wasn't."

"You just ran away?" His wife looked hurt.

Roselmann told her, "We'll get to that. Dr. Samra, suppose you tell them what happened."

The professor cleared his throat, then proceeded to tell his astonishing story. "About a month before I went to the Middle East, a former student visited me in Cape May. I was surprised when he mentioned working for the CIA. Mind you, he was pleasant enough, but not my best scholar. I forget what kind of grades he got."

He silently struggled to remember. Heather felt encouraged by how normal he sounded.

"Nevertheless," he went on, "I mentioned my upcoming Middle East study trip. He lectured me about the dangers and asked if I'd considered the risks. I assured him I had." The older professor inhaled deeply. "Suddenly he changed his tune and asked for my assistance. Since I'm originally from Lebanon, he thought I could blend in easily. Naturally I protested."

"You worked for the CIA!" Heather exclaimed.

"Now, you'd better allow me to explain, child," he began motioning with his thick hands. "It isn't at all the way it sounds."

Dr. Samra paused to collect his wits. "My former student said he was working on finding missing Americans in the Middle East. If I would try to determine their whereabouts, he promised to arrange interviews with leading terrorists. After much consideration, I agreed to help him—but not for the sake of my new book. I wanted to do something for my country."

Heather looked deeply into his sad gray eyes. *He doesn't sound as if the mission were successful,* she thought.

"He said a top CIA Middle East man would contact me. Two days later, I drove to Philadelphia and met that man in center city. It was Jeremy Ponereau. He too was a former student at Kirby College."

He let that news sink in as his wife gasped, then proceeded. "He instructed me to pose as a Lebanese reporter sympathetic to the terrorist leaders. Believe me, that was difficult!" he exclaimed. "The meetings had to be handled delicately and, as a result, didn't occur until the end of my tour. Just days before I left, Ponereau called and told me what to do. At the appointed time, I met a major terrorist. I don't feel free to reveal all I learned, but I will tell what relates to the Council for Democracy meeting."

"Is that when you first heard about it?" Chief Cullen asked.

"That is correct."

Heather waited excitedly for the history professor to answer her many questions.

"What Mr. Ponereau did not count on was a certain bonus meeting I had with a very talkative terrorist. He told me astonishing things about the young agent. In fact, he talked even more than me, and that's saying something!"

Nervous laughter rippled like a refreshing wave across the room. Heather realized she hadn't laughed in days.

"I learned Ponereau's sympathies lie with whatever terrorist group pays him the most."

Heather said, "I didn't think he was that bad!"

The history professor nodded. "He's been given a large sum to stop that conference tomorrow. If it goes on, several terror groups will be put out of business. I can't say more about that, but I do know the CIA Director is to be killed so the meeting won't go on."

Officer Armgard let out a low whistle of concern.

"That's the extent of my information about the meeting," the professor concluded. "I haven't slept much for thinking about it."

"Amazing!" Heather exclaimed. "But I still don't understand why you disappeared."

Dr. Samra shook his head. "That terrorist leader must have discovered who I really was. You see, right before I left, I received a death threat. The next day someone blew up the car I had rented."

"Oh, George!" Mrs. Samra exclaimed.

He hung his head. "I was nowhere close to the car. But six people who happened to be passing by were seriously injured in the blast."

No one knew quite what to say.

"On my way back to the States, I was so afraid a bomb had been planted on the plane and would take more innocent lives. . . . I knew I had to think of some way to handle this that wouldn't hurt anyone else."

He buried his head in his hands. A few moments later he went on.

"Maybe I did not make the wisest choices, but no one else has been harmed. That was my only concern. When you're dealing with terrorists, you can never be sure what they might do. I figured if they found me alone, at least they wouldn't hurt my family. I also wrestled over how to disclose Ponereau's identity as a double agent."

"I think you did the right thing, Professor," Chief Cullen declared.

"When I left those computer disks at home, I prayed you'd find them, Heather. I knew you could get into the files, but I worried so that you'd be endangered. This has been very stressful." His shoulders sagged.

"I'm honored you chose me," Heather said quietly.

"My idea was to hide until tonight," he said. "That way my disappearance would distract Ponereau for a while. Mr. Roselmann tells me that Hal Morgan created another distraction when he tried to steal my book." Dr. Samra shook his shaggy gray head. "We never should have hired the man."

"I'm relieved your plan worked," Mrs. Samra said, squeezing his hand affectionately.

Roselmann summed up the professor's story. "Somehow Ponereau is going to assassinate the CIA Director."

"Either he'll do it or someone else will," Dr. Samra responded.

"We certainly have our work cut out for us, don't we?" Roselmann sighed. "I'll personally warn the Director. Chief, how about putting the professor under a heavy guard in a motel? Dr. and Mrs. Samra, I know this will be difficult, but you shouldn't stay together tonight or let your children know what's happening until this is over. No doubt Ponereau's looking high and low for you to make sure you don't blow his plot."

"I fully understand," he said.

"I do too," his wife answered bravely.

Chief Cullen said gruffly, "Weaver, you come with me and the professor. Armgard, take the Reeds and Mrs. Samra back home and stay with them tonight. Holmes is shadowing Ponereau. Carry on."

# 17

## Nightmare

On the way home, though it was almost one-thirty, they talked excitedly about the professor's return.

"I wonder how Ponereau's going to attempt that assassination," Heather worried.

"He's pretty crafty," her father noted. "I'll bet the plot is well-planned."

"You know what makes me nervous?" Officer Armgard asked. "That guy's working with terrorists. If he's counting on a group of them to back him up tomorrow. . ."

"How far do you think he'd go?" the sixteen-year-old inquired.

"I wouldn't put anything past that guy," the policeman responded. "You heard the professor say what he's like." When Mrs. Reed gasped, he tried to sound more hopeful. "I'm sure Officer Holmes will find out what he's up to. He's topnotch."

When Heather finally got to bed, she found she was too agitated to sleep. The teenager went downstairs and found Armgard wide awake too.

"Would you like some hot chocolate?" she offered.

"Yeah, that would be nice," he said.

They enjoyed a friendly discussion about the case and before long, she felt sleepy enough to go back to bed. As Heather rinsed out their cups and started putting them in the dishwasher, the phone rang.

Armgard automatically picked it up. "Oh, hi, Pete. What's up?" he said.

Heather listened closely to his side of the conversation.

"What did Holmes find out? He did?" The officer scratched his chin. Then, "Man alive! Yep. Bye."

"What is it?" Heather asked anxiously.

"That was Pete Roselmann. An hour ago, Holmes followed Ponereau to an all-night restaurant. He was with a man who looked like a Middle Easterner."

"Wow! Could he hear them?" Her eyes glowed with anticipation.

"Yeah, they were talking about tomorrow's pow-wow at the Council for Democracy. Holmes overheard Ponereau's sidekick say, 'Everything has been taken care of. No one will ever suspect.'"

"He's so slick," Heather said in disgust. The thought of Ponereau's betrayal stung once again.

"I agree. Anyway, you'd better get some sleep," he advised.

"I can only try," she responded, once again feeling wide awake.

The petite girl climbed the stairs to her room and crawled into bed. Even Murgatroid was active at that late hour. Finally weariness led Heather to sleep—and nightmares.

In the last one Jeremy Ponereau and a group of ruthless, black-hooded terrorists with automatic weapons engaged her in a horrifying car chase. When her vehicle ran out of gas, Heather found herself cornered with no way of escape. Ponereau slowly stalked toward her, wearing an evil expression of revenge on his face. His accomplices followed on his heels. Then the CIA agent finally confronted Heather, his eyes aglow with hatred. He reached inside his coat for a pistol and struck her viciously across the face with it. The teenager fell in a heap at his feet as Ponereau snarled at his companions, "Finish the job."

Heather screamed.

"Wake up! You're having a bad dream." Mrs. Reed sat on the bed and gently shook her daughter. "Come on, sweetheart—wake up."

The sixteen-year-old slowly climbed out of sleep and found herself shivering.

"It's all right now," her mother's soft voice soothed. "You're safe." Then she waited a moment while Heather cleared sleep cobwebs from her brain.

"Do you want to tell me about it?" Mrs. Reed asked kindly, stroking her daughter's moist brow.

"Oh, Mom, it was awful! Jeremy Ponereau and a bunch of terrorists chased me. When my car ran out of gas, he hit me with his gun and told his buddies to finish me off."

"That is terrible!" her mother exclaimed. "But it's no wonder you dreamed like that considering what's happened around here."

Heather suddenly noticed her mother's golden hair was slightly damp, and she was already dressed. "What time is it?"

"Six-thirty," she smiled. "Time to get up."

Heather sniffed and sat up. "Um, smells good. I am hungry, even after that nightmare."

"Good! Miriam is making something delicious," Mrs. Reed said.

Heather quickly showered and dressed, then selected a red wool skirt and matching sweater. Downstairs she found her parents, Mrs. Samra and the police officer waiting for her.

"You could've started without me," she told them.

"No problem, dear," her father responded. As soon as he said a blessing over the food, Mrs. Reed said, "Jenn came by ten minutes ago to pick you up for school. I told her you were running late."

"Did you tell her Dr. Samra came home?" she asked eagerly.

"No. We thought it would be best to wait."

Just then the phone rang.

"I'll get it!" Heather jumped up. "Oh, hello, Chief Cullen. Yes, he's here." Turning to the hungry-looking policeman, she said, "Chief Cullen wants to talk to you."

Armgard sighed, pushed his chair away from the table and took the phone. "Good morning, Chief."

They all listened curiously to the one-sided conversation. No one ate. About five minutes later, the officer hung up. "The Chief wants me at the station in ten minutes," he reported.

Heather was somewhat surprised. "What about us?"

"Don't we need you anymore?" Mrs. Reed asked.

"It's not that," he explained. "But I have to go elsewhere. Officer Weaver will be covering you now."

"How about eating first?" Mrs. Reed suggested.

He grinned. "I guess I have enough time for that."

While he dug into a stack of fluffy pancakes, Heather picked at hers, troubled by a persistent thought. Finally she asked, "How will we find out what happens?"

Armgard took a big gulp of coffee and looked her in the eye. "You've been in on this case from the start, haven't you?" She nodded. "Now we want you to step aside just as it's about to break wide open. I'll tell you what. When it's all over, I'll personally fill you in, okay?"

Heather forced a polite smile, though she felt far from pleased. Armgard left moments later.

Mr. Reed regarded the clock anxiously. "I'm going to be late for my staff meeting if I don't get moving," he announced.

"Dad, I'm running behind, too, and don't have a car," said Heather. "Could I drop you off at the train and borrow yours?"

"Good thinking!" he praised her. "Grab your things, and let's be on our way!"

When they reached the Kirby passenger station, the

teenager kissed her dad good-bye and drove off. Two blocks later, Heather had another one of her brainstorms and suddenly turned and headed away from Kirby High and straight toward the Council for Democracy!

# 18

## Rescue

It took Heather forty-five minutes to weed through rush hour traffic. When she neared Valley Forge National Park, the teenager pulled off the expressway onto the road leading to the Council for Democracy.

On the radio a newscaster mentioned the important meeting. *"This morning a critical conference on Middle East terrorism will take place at the Council for Democracy. Top international officials will attend, including CIA Director Robert Mulholland. Security is very tight."*

Everything appeared to be going normally, but Heather knew better. She pulled into the tree-lined entrance that led to the modern, glass and chrome structure with its underground parking garage. An outdoor sidewalk with more trees wrapped itself around the exterior of the building. Police cars and vans were all over the place.

Heather pulled up to the parking garage and was immediately stopped by a tough-looking guard.

"Where's your pass?" he snapped.

"W-what pass?" Heather stammered.

His eyes narrowed. "State your business."

She found herself blurting out, "I'm working with Peter Roselmann of the FBI."

"So where's your pass?" he challenged.

"I wasn't issued a special one," she admitted.

"Then you'll have to go to the far end of the building where there's regular parking," he instructed.

Heather breathed a sigh of relief as she put the car in reverse. *He must be admitting the top officials,* she guessed. *Somehow I've got to get back to that garage. That seems to be where all the action is.*

She steered her dad's car to a ground-level lot where security wasn't as tight. Tense-looking men and women hurried to get to work on time. A peek at her watch told Heather it was now eight-forty-five.

Trying to look as though she belonged, she followed a group of women into an elevator. *Am I ever glad I dressed up today!* she thought. *I must not call attention to myself.*

She hoped Roselmann and his colleagues had taken the necessary steps to protect these innocent lives. *Imagine if they knew what was really going on!* she shivered.

When she got out of the elevator, Heather nearly blew her cover. She tripped over a potted fern and dropped her purse. The teen's lipstick rolled across the floor, and a dignified man slid on it. For a moment, time stood still as the man almost crash landed in some ferns.

Fortunately no one seemed to notice that Heather was responsible for the near accident. So she just pretended to be an innocent bystander while all the attention was being focused on the startled executive.

Now she scanned her surroundings carefully, looking for a way to get back to the parking garage. A gruff looking watchman with a thick facial scar stood by a stairwell. *I'd rather get caught by a pit bull,* she thought. *And I'll bet those stairs lead to the garage! How will I ever get past him?*

Heather checked her watch, trying to look as if she were waiting for someone. Out of the corner of her eye, she spotted a well-dressed man take the guard aside. His back was to the door now, and the other man looked off to the side, away from Heather.

*Here's my chance!* she thought, tension spreading through her body. She stealthily slid past a row of rubber trees, which hid her from their view. Then she gently pushed open the door and hurried down the stairs. Heather was feeling pleased with herself until she collided with Mike Armgard at the bottom of the steps! He was not pleased.

"What in tarnation are YOU doing here?" he yelled.

Heather stuttered, "Please don't make me go back! I'll get arrested if that guard finds me."

"Heather, you could get yourself killed hanging around here," he bellowed. "We're dealing with international terrorists, not movie thugs."

He scratched his stubbled chin trying to figure out what to do with her. Just then, a familiar voice came over his walkie talkie.

Heather heard a man say, "Armgard, Roselmann here. Go to the south side of the garage. Ponereau's on his way."

"Over!" the officer responded. "Heather Reed, I'd like to take you and . . . oh, forget it! Get into my squad car." He pointed toward his cruiser twenty feet away. "And for goodness' sake, stay there!"

"Oh, thank you," Heather gushed. She dashed toward the vehicle and climbed into the backseat. The combination of suspense and having a bird's-eye view left her feeling giddy. The teenager guessed she would be among the first to spot Jeremy Ponereau's car as he drove into the heavily-guarded area. The place swarmed with law enforcement officials, some in plain clothes.

As she looked around, Heather noticed a large truck with a flat-bed trailer. A container the size of a small car rested on it. *I wonder what that is?* she asked herself.

Heather began to shiver in the cold squad car. But she quickly forgot her discomfort when Ponereau's car appeared at the entrance. She watched as the guard checked his pass and waved him inside. To her surprise the agent parked just five cars away! Heather crouched down to avoid detection.

Jeremy Ponereau got out of his car and reached back inside for a briefcase. When he shut the door, he looked around nervously.

*He's not very composed,* Heather observed. *I wonder if there are terrorists backing him up nearby?*

The CIA agent had taken only a few steps when Peter Roselmann's voice boomed over a loudspeaker: "Stop right where you are, Ponereau!"

The events that followed hit with hurricane-force speed. Ponereau drew a gun from inside his black wool coat. Then shots rang out from another direction, and the CIA agent slumped against his car.

Heather was horrified. *Is he dead?* she thought wildly.

Two people, dressed like astronauts, and a dog from the K-9 corps burst out of the truck she had noticed earlier. The German Shepherd sniffed the agent's car and began barking furiously. One of the men yelled, "I found a live one! Evacuate!"

Within minutes people began streaming from the main part of the building. Police and special agents moved into position as the trailer pulled next to Ponereau's vehicle.

*That must be for deactivating bombs!* Heather thought. *I wish someone would move Ponereau out of the way!*

Before she knew what she was doing, Heather burst out of the car and raced toward Ponereau. No one paid attention at first. Then Roselmann spotted her and shouted from the other side of the garage, "Heather, get out of here!"

But she didn't hear him. With a rush of adrenaline she grabbed Jeremy Ponereau's ice-cold hands and dragged him toward the entrance. People fleeing from the building stopped to watch the drama. Heather was mindless of them. A TV cameraman there to film the arrival of the CIA Director recorded the scene from a safe distance.

Paramedics took over when Heather got outside the garage. They lifted Ponereau's limp body into their vehicle. Two government agent types climbed in with him, and the ambulance sped off with the siren screaming.

Suddenly there was a loud explosion. That's when physical effort and mental strain ganged up on Heather. Everything began to swirl. Her legs went weak and crumpled under her. Then her head hit something hard.

# 19

## Revelations

Heather moaned as her hazel eyes began to focus. She was on the family room couch.

"She's waking up!" her father exclaimed.

Mrs. Reed checked her daughter's pulse. "How are you feeling, honey?"

"My head hurts," she complained. "What's going on?"

Brian, Dr. and Mrs. Samra, Officers Armgard and Weaver, and Peter Roselmann stood nearby. Were they going to yell at her for getting into trouble again?

"I brought you home," Armgard answered.

"Oh," she mumbled. "What time is it?"

"One o'clock," her mother said. "You fainted, then hit your head."

It all slowly began coming back to her. "There was an explosion." She shivered, afraid to know what had happened next.

Roselmann explained as Brian handed her a cup of hot tea. "The bomb squad discharged the device in a special bin without a moment to spare. That was the explosion you heard. They also discovered several other bombs, including one in the CIA Director's temporary quarters. They were all discovered in time."

"Thank God!" she expressed. "Is the Director all right?"

"Just fine. He was escorted to the conference after the shouting was over," the agent explained. "I guess we got lucky."

"More than luck was at work here, son," Dr. Samra corrected.

"What about Ponereau?" Heather asked groggily.

"I don't know why you're so concerned with that creep," Brian mumbled in disgust.

Roselmann ignored the remark. "He's in stable condition at King of Prussia Hospital. He got hit twice, once in the shoulder, then in the left leg."

"Why did you risk your life to save him after all he's done?" Brian asked. "He's not worth the trouble."

Heather searched her brother's eyes and saw more than anger reflected in them. Then she looked at Dr. Samra and wondered how he felt about what she had done. His smile told her what she wanted to know: he understood.

"I'm really not sure why I did it," she admitted. "I knew he was a jerk, and I was furious with him." She paused. "But I didn't want him to get blown up."

"Maybe she gets that from me," her mother smiled gently.

"That's right," Heather said. "I've heard you say a thousand times, 'All life is precious.'" She rested for a

moment then inquired, "What about the terrorists working with Ponereau? Were they caught?"

"Not yet," Roselmann admitted. "But we're working
on a few leads. We think the fellow Ponereau met last
night was his only associate on this job—at least on this
side of the ocean."

"I believe I know just who that man is," Dr. Samra
reflected. "I'd be happy to help you find him."

"Thank you, Professor. I'll definitely take you up on
that," Roselmann said. "In the meantime, you'll be under
constant protection until we find the guy."

"I'm so happy this terrible ordeal is almost over," said
Mrs. Samra. She smiled sweetly into her husband's warm
eyes, and he hugged her.

Heather grinned broadly. Then her smile quickly
faded.

"How much trouble am I in for skipping school and
going to the Council for Democracy?" she asked, know-
ing she would have to pay the consequences.

"Don't forget to include taking my car under false
pretenses," her father added with mock sternness. "But
we'll discuss that later."

Then it was Roselmann's turn. "I am more than a little
annoyed with you for going to the Council for Democracy. You could have ruined everything. Just think of the
danger you put yourself in and possibly others, as well.
On the other hand, you were a big help earlier because
you discovered Ponereau was bad news." Then he
smiled. "I don't think we'll give you any trouble."

"But I may," Mrs. Reed added with a twinkle in her eyes.

When the laughter died down, Mr. Reed said, "We're in demand again."

"Huh?" Heather asked.

"The press. It's a zoo on the front lawn." He tilted his head toward the front of the house.

"What do they want now?" his son asked.

Mr. Reed imitated a television newsman. "A Middle East expert prevents disaster at The Council for Democracy as teenage hero saves crooked CIA agent from doom. Story at eleven."

"I'll go talk to them," Dr. Samra said pleasantly, getting up from his seat. Suddenly he hesitated. "Mr. Roselmann, is it all right for me to talk to the press?"

The FBI agent thought for a moment. "You can tell them you're back safe and sound but no more. We haven't closed this case just yet."

"I hear you," the professor said.

"They can just wait until you're strong enough to be interviewed young lady," her mother said sternly. "You've already over-taxed yourself."

Heather had to agree. But before the officers left, she told Peter Roselmann she wanted to visit Ponereau at the hospital.

"Whatever for?" He raised his eyebrows.

"I want to know why he became a double agent. Like, what were his motives? And I also want him to know I've forgiven him."

"Forgiven him?" Roselmann sniffed. "That guy is no good, Heather. He doesn't deserve it."

"Maybe not, but it's important to me that I tell him I'm not bitter," she said softly.

Her mother overheard them and commented, "That's the mark of a true hero."

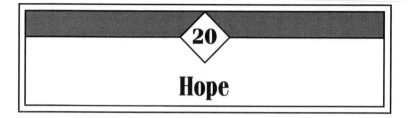

# Hope

eather slept for four hours. After that and a roast-beef dinner, she felt quite well. Roselmann and Officer Weaver picked her up at seven to visit Jeremy Ponereau. The FBI agent was in a happy mood.

"We got the guy working with Ponereau!" he announced as the Reeds gathered around him in the foyer.

"That's wonderful!" Patrick Reed exclaimed.

"How did you do it?" his wife inquired.

"Dr. Samra gave us some good information about him. He also remembered what the guy's part was to be this morning."

"What was that?" Heather asked excitedly.

"After bombing the place, he planned to hustle out of town on the next flight," he said. "We arrested him at the airport."

"That's terrific!" she exclaimed.

"What was Ponereau supposed to do?" Brian asked.

Roselmann grinned. "Maybe Heather can find that out."

The teenager grabbed her brown leather flight jacket from the hall closet. "Let's get going!"

But first she took a few minutes to speak with reporters who still waited on her front lawn. When they arrived at the King of Prussia Hospital, the trio rode the elevator to the sixth floor. Ponereau was in a guarded room where he had been moved following surgery.

"Don't be too disappointed if he doesn't want to talk to you," Roselmann cautioned. "He does have his rights."

"I understand," she said.

Roselmann told the police guard who they were and what they wanted. The officer quickly unlocked the door.

Heather entered quietly. The curtains were drawn, and the only light in the room came from a lamp over Ponereau's bed. He turned slowly as the door closed and was amazed to find the girl he had double-crossed standing there. He stared for a moment, then looked away.

She carefully approached his bed, avoiding the IV pole and tubes connected to his arm. He looked drained.

"How are you feeling?" Heather asked awkwardly.

He disregarded the small talk. "I heard what you did for me."

"I know you don't have to talk to me," she said, "but I'd like to know why you planted those bombs. You could've blown yourself up too, you know."

He stared at her. "No, I wouldn't."

"Oh! So you'd get out safely while others got hurt or killed?"

"More or less," he murmured.

"I don't understand that at all!" she said harshly.

"You wouldn't," he remarked.

"Why do you say that?"

"Because you're very different from me."

Heather tried to be patient. "Would you mind explaining that?"

"You trust people," he said simply.

"I guess you don't."

He shook his head. "But I didn't always feel that way."

"What happened?" she asked.

He inhaled deeply. "Do you really want to know?"

"Yes, and besides, you owe me," she smiled slyly.

He sniffed and shook his head. "You drive a hard bargain. Very well, I'll tell you, but it isn't nice."

"I'm listening," she said, pulling up a chair and crossing her arms.

"I joined the CIA ten years ago. They sent me to the Middle East five years later. My partner, Paul Nathans, and I were in the anti-terrorism unit. About a year ago, the Director ordered him to go underground."

"Mr. Mulholland?" Heather interrupted.

Ponereau scowled. "Yes."

"And by underground do you mean pretend he was really on the terrorists' side?" she asked.

He nodded. "The Director promised to protect Paul. But he lied," the agent clenched his teeth. "Mulholland abandoned Paul the minute his identity was uncovered."

There was no mistaking the hostility in the agent's voice.

"What happened to him?" Heather asked gently.

"The terrorists tortured Paul for a week, then killed him," Ponereau blurted. "I wanted revenge." He gazed at the wall silently for a short time. Heather hoped he'd finish the tragic story. Presently, he continued.

"I arranged to do the job during that Council for Democracy meeting," he said vaguely. Heather realized he wasn't about to tell all.

"I planned to get the Director safely out of the building after the first bomb went off. Then someone else would shoot him."

The teenager added, "And no one would ever know because you would be a hero. It would look like your life was in danger too."

Ponereau smiled thinly. "I always knew you were sharp."

"Dr. Samra's disappearance got in the way of your plan, didn't it?" she pursued.

"That was designed to throw me off, wasn't it?" he asked. Heather nodded. "Did he ever show up?"

"Yes, he did. And guess what? Your plan failed after I found a clue in the computer file that I didn't tell you about."

She told Ponereau about Dr. Samra's clever message in the Lord's Prayer. Then Heather mentioned the professor's reappearance the night before and Officer Holmes' discovery at the restaurant. Ponereau lay still, thinking hard. She repeated, "Why did you plant a bomb in your car?"

A distressed look flashed across the agent's face. "I didn't," he told her. "My colleague tricked me. I only wanted to kill the Director, not a whole bunch of people, and certainly not myself. You can't trust anyone," he concluded.

"Maybe not everyone," she corrected, "but that's no reason to write off the human race."

A nurse entered with the agent's pain medication.

"I guess this is good-bye," Heather remarked.

Ponereau held up a hand to stop her. "Before you go, I want to thank you for saving my life." Then he hesitated before saying, "I am sorry you couldn't trust me."

Heather smiled. "I forgive you."

Ponereau became confused. "You do? Why?"

"I mess up a lot in other ways, but God always forgives me," she said humbly. "And He can forgive you too. Maybe you'll let me explain it to you someday."

When Heather got home, she was surprised to find a party in progress. The family room was filled with people—Brian and her parents, Dr. and Mrs. Samra and their four children (three of whom had flown in from different parts of the country), Jenn McLaughlin, and Dick Walker. Peter Roselmann, Chief Cullen and Officers Armgard, Weaver, and Holmes were also on hand. Everyone congratulated Heather for solving the mystery.

"Thank you," she said modestly. "I owe a lot to Dr. Samra, my brother, and Jenn."

At one point her father motioned her into his study. A reporter from his paper had come to interview her.

"How would you sum up the adventure you just had?" she asked.

"It was a little scary," said Heather. "But it was also thrilling to be able to help. And I learned a lot that will help me the next time a mystery comes along."

The teenager's father simply sighed.

# ABOUT THE AUTHOR

Rebecca Price Janney has dual careers as both a writer and a teacher. As a freelance writer, she has had numerous articles published in newspapers and magazines, including *Seventeen, Decision, Moody Monthly, World Vision, Childlife, War Cry,* and *The Young Salvationist.* Her published work also includes a section in *Shaped by God's Love,* an anthology published by World Wide Publishers. As a teacher at Cabrini College, her speciality is Jewish and Middle East History. Rebecca and her husband Scott live in suburban Philadelphia.

*Four new, exciting whodunits!*

# THE HEATHER REED SERIES

It's no mystery why this series is catching on! Heather Reed is a sixteen-year-old with an uncanny ability to be in the right place at the wrong time. Her unquenchable curiosity guarantees suspense-filled, mystery adventures young readers will want to read over and over again.

### #1—The Cryptic Clue

When the Reed's next-door neighbor, a famous history professor, mysteriously disappears, Heather is determined to find out what happened, but her curiosity brings her within a heartbeat of tragedy. A hidden clue draws her into the nerve center of a vengeful international plot.

### #2—The Model Mystery

Top competitors in The American Model of the Year Contest have received anonymous threats. Heather Reed decides to try her hand at reporting for a popular teenage magazine—what better way to find out why a beauty competition has suddenly turned ugly? But before she can reveal the culprits' prideful plot, Heather and her best friend find themselves in serious danger.

### #3—The Eerie Echo

During a student tour to Israel, Heather soon finds out that not everything in the Holy Land is holy. A mystery soon unfolds that involves mysterious catacombs, a haunted church, a missing French ambassador, and a priceless Christian artifact.

### #4—The Toxic Secret

When a well-known environmental activist receives death threats and becomes gravely ill, sixteen-year-old amateur detective Heather Reed deciphers the strange and intriguing facts. This suspenseful whodunit combines old-fashioned mystery with issues that are important to today's young readers.

*Don't miss this funny new series from WORDKids!*

# THE INCREDIBLE WORLDS OF WALLY McDOOGLE
## by Bill Myers

### #1—My Life As a Smashed Burrito with Extra Hot Sauce

Twelve-year-old Wally—"The walking disaster area"—is forced to stand up to Camp Wahkah Wahkah's number one all-American bad guy. One hilarious mishap follows another until, fighting together for their very lives, Wally learns the need for even his worst enemy to receive Jesus Christ. (ISBN 0–8499–3402–8)

### #2—My Life As Alien Monster Bait

"Hollyweird" comes to Middletown! Wally's a superstar! A movie company has chosen our hero to be eaten by their mechanical "Mutant from Mars!" It's a close race as to which will consume Wally first—the disaster-plagued special effects "monster" or his own out-of-control pride . . . until he learns the cost of true friendship and of God's command for humility. (ISBN 0–8499–3403–6)

### #3—My Life As a Broken Bungee Cord

A hot-air balloon race! What could be more fun? Then again, we're talking about Wally McDoogle, the "Human Catastrophe." Calamity builds on calamity until, with his life on the line, Wally learns what it means to FULLY put his trust in God. (ISBN 0–8499–3404–4)

### #4—My Life As Crocodile Junk Food

Wally visits missionary friends in the South American rain forest. Here he stumbles onto a whole new set of impossible predicaments . . . until he understands the need and joy of sharing Jesus Christ with others. (ISBN 0–8499–3405–2)

**Look for this humorous fiction series at your local Christian bookstore.**